Growing Up Hollywood

A Short Story Collection

TARA BOTEL DOHERTY

Copyright © 2019 by Tara Botel Doherty

All rights reserved. No part of this publication may be reproduced, distributed or transmitted in any form or by any means, including photocopying, recording, or other electronic or mechanical methods, without the prior written permission of the publisher, except in the case of brief quotations embodied in critical reviews and certain other noncommercial uses permitted by copyright law. For permission requests, write to the publisher, addressed "Attention: Permissions Coordinator," at the address below.

Pinehurst Literary Press

Cover Art by Jessica Barnes
Cover Design by Emma Michaels
Interior Design by Laurisa Reyes

Hardcover ISBN: 978-0-9984647-4-9
Paperback ISBN: 978-0-9984647-3-2

Publisher's Note: This is a work of fiction. Names, characters, places, and incidents are a product of the author's imagination. Locales and public names are sometimes used for atmospheric purposes. Any resemblance to actual people, living or dead, or to businesses, companies, events, institutions, or locales is completely coincidental.

"All happy families are alike; each unhappy family is unhappy in its own way."
- Leo Tolstoy in *Anna Karenina*

Table of Contents

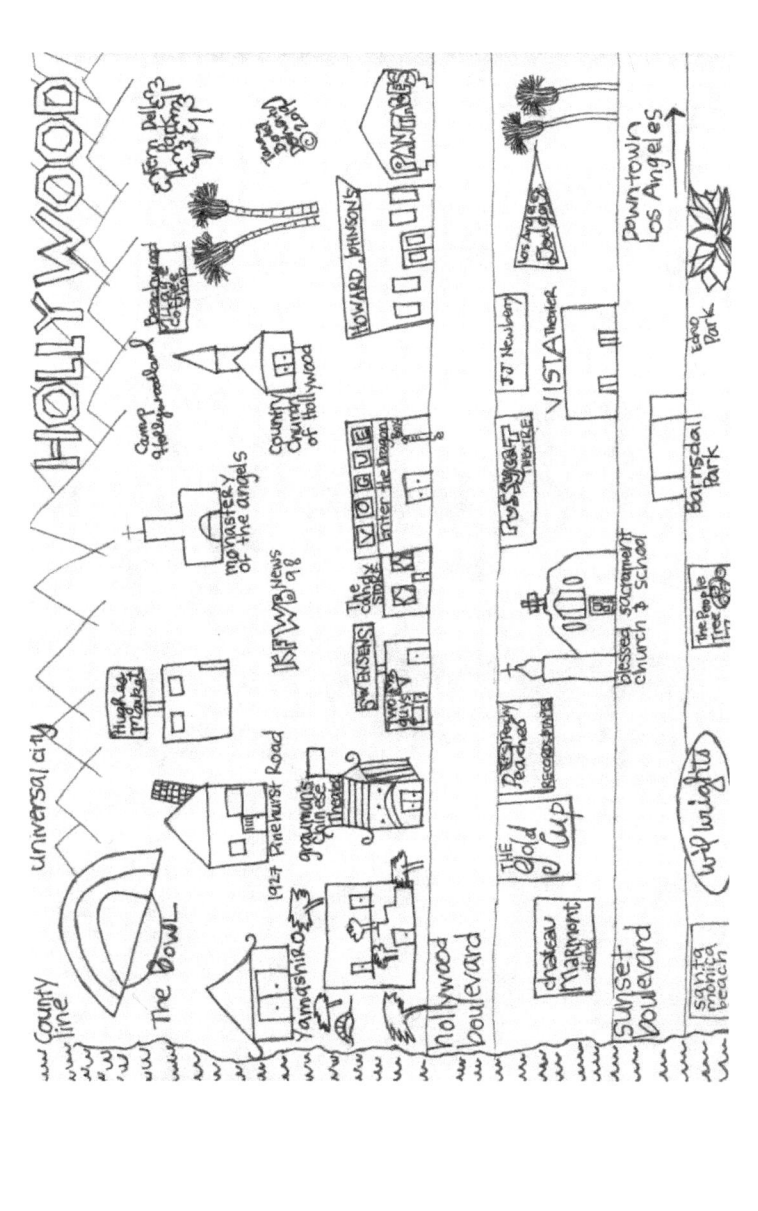

Once Upon A Time in Hollywood

Once upon a time in Hollywood, I'm going to have a husband who loves me more than anything and a bunch of children who will be as graceful and beautiful as I am. We will live so high up in the Hollywood Hills that the palm trees will look like dandelions from our Olympus. My Prince will work in the studios and I will bring his cocktail out to the kidney shaped pool in our sprawling ranch style house where the growing Los Angeles skyline will appear to be just beyond our backyard. It will be that rare day when the smog has not attached itself to the civic center and the offshore winds are blowing. The perfect picture. We will be the white-bordered frame of perfection in our 1960's snapshot. Post war. Post troubles. Post post.

"Union Station-ten minutes," the conductor announced through the loud speaker. She had finally arrived. The perfection of a downtown Los Angeles afternoon left Mia in the style of excitement that was reminiscent of innocent children on Christmas morning.

"You can't live in the past. This is 1960, you'll be able to have more children," was the last thing the doctor said to her before she left the hotel room. Mia felt relieved. She watched the fluorescent lights flicker from the oversized table lamp with a pulsating hum. Never going to let there be a repeat performance. No encores, she kept mouthing to herself in a repetitive prayer. Taking off the sheet, she swore to only laugh and play the piano.

Mia would never let a man take something from her again. She would be in charge from now on. To be a modern, independent woman would be her goal. To be a thinker and an artist had always been her way, but now she was not so sure about her future. The United States was in a Cold War with Russia and everyone was on edge. War seemed the inevitable outcome in this post-World War II world. From now on, Mia would get what she wanted because she would want what she got.

Mia had tried to remember all the directions that had been given to her. Fever. Infection. Bleeding. Discomfort. Hospital. Doctor. None of it was retained because she refused to accept those thoughts. She would only think nice thoughts in the story of her life.

This was the land of futures and second acts. Mia could reinvent herself. In the land of make believe, smoke and mirrors, she was certain of only one thing — herself, Mia. She could only rely on herself from this day forward. No promises. No long choruses and questionable people. No powerlessness. Life could all be different now. She was in control.

Mia took a taxi to that small California bungalow she had shared with her mother for decades. It had been ten years since her father, Richard, had been found dead in his chair on the front porch. The two of them again would live together, but now she was a woman who could make her own choices. She would be more careful this time. Mia would be in charge.

In the backseat of the Yellow Cab, she rode past all of the shops and homes along Sunset Boulevard. Hats. Dresses. Ceramic Bauer bowls that contributed to the modern look like a perfect lamp or table of concentric circles in a Case Study House. As she rode along in the taxi, the feelings of homecoming and belonging washed over her. Through the opened window, the dry heat filled the air. The City of Angels had been the only place where she had truly felt comfortable. She was protected by the angels who watched over her throughout her life. If Mia had never left this city she loved so much, then perhaps the attack might not have happened. She would and could never allow this to happen again.

Six months ago, Mia was playing at a piano bar on Vermont Avenue in Hollywood. It was her last night before she went on a piano tour of the lower states. She was so excited; her trunk was packed full of costumes she and her mother had sewn. She had saved money for an overnight bag so that she would have a quick change of clothes for a show. When she touched those keys, her soul opened up and through the notes on the sheet, all was revealed through her heart and her head. The piano was the story of her life. It was all she had and all she wanted.

"Mia, you still play so beautifully."

Lost in her own thoughts, she heard him but did not stop. Finally, the piece was finished. The notes stopped. Mia turned around to see him. She had not seen Father Michael in years. The last time was when Mia graduated from eighth grade at St. Francis. He had been transferred in when she was in the seventh grade. He brought a fresh take on the Catholic Church, and a fresh take on male beauty. Young, good looking and interested in her, that was what Father Michael had brought to the church for her. She had never experienced an adult interested in what she had to say and when she said it. He looked like a prince from her fairy tales. She remembered his long, dark eyelashes and his twinkling, cobalt blue eyes. They were blue outlined with

4

hazel and a dot on the right side of his right eye. It had been difficult to stay focused during that last year, but she had been successful. She could easily have fallen in love with Father Michael, but he was already committed.

She stayed away from the church when she realized her feelings for him. There were a few celebrations that brought her back. Participating in May Procession with Mary, the Mother of God and all of the crowns on the altar brought her into the church, but she still stayed away from him. Most importantly was her Confirmation, which was confirming her promise to God, the Pope, and the Roman Catholic Church. She affirmed and confirmed, but more importantly she stayed away from him because she felt such a strange magnetic pull to Father Michael.

"The ten years have been wonderful to you. You still have your gift. Truly you are so talented, I always knew you would be a star," stated Father Michael.

He was in his collar. Still magically handsome. Those twinkling blue eyes with a few more lines, even more when he smiled.

"Father Michael, so good to see you," she said with her hand extended. He quickly shook her hand and released it. Her arm felt like a rag doll at the side of her body, limp from the lack of attention. The moment of silence was interrupted by a second man clearing his throat.

Father Michael stepped back.

"Yes, Mia. This is Freddy, my little brother. He likes to be called Red. I call him Frederick when he is not behaving himself."

Mia was confused, she had been introduced to Red years ago by Father Michael on the church steps. She never forgot the tune he whispered in her ear, from a Dean Martin song. Perhaps that was why every performance she gave had a Rat Pack song. His closeness to her young body was a happy memory.

"Yes, I met you years ago on the stairs. Nice to see you, again," Mia said with a small laugh. She looked down at his shoes, shiny black dress shoes. As her eyes moved upward, from his shiny patent leathers to his dress whites, she recognized his stand. He was still as handsome as the first time she saw him.

Red stepped in a little too close to her. He leaned into her piano bench and put out his hand to greet her.

Mia recalled Red singing to her years ago, but at the time she was a bit alarmed by the lyrics. In her imagination she thought the title was "Stay with Me." She was flattered by his attention, but dismayed that this older guy was so forward as to sing he wanted her to stay the night with him. Only later when she heard Dean Martin sing "Sway" did she realize Red had made up the lyrics. The original words were so much more suggestive. Red's words were right for her and she liked them so much better.

"Da da da da da da da da da,
Long before love sits in,
Take my love and go and take it now,
Stay with me, Da da da."

She really wished she could get to know Red better, but her timing was always off. She was about to go on her tour, to fulfill her dreams of playing, performing, and living.

"Girly, get back to the keys. This may be your last night, but you are still on the clock. It's not time for your break yet!" Carl the owner of the piano bar, physically turned her body back around. Mia conceded and got back to her microphone. She was in a confused haze, she was in a state of Red. Carl had no trouble touching things and people who were not related to him or belonged to him. He had the ability to ruin the moment.

"We'll let you go," said Father Michael, obviously embarrassed by Red's behavior.

"It was great to see you again, Father Michael," said Mia.

"Nice to see you again, Red," Mia said, sorry not to have the song continue. She knew that Red was interested in her, like all of the other boys and men she had known. When he stood next to her and whispered in her ear all of those years ago, she felt a connection.

So, she turned around getting back to her bench, moving the starched lace of her crinoline skirt. Being the center of attention at the piano demanded a formal cocktail dress. A

Christian Dior "New Look" knock-off from Lerner's on the Boulevard. She loved the tight crunch of the starched lace and petticoats sound as she sat on her piano bench, speaking gently into the microphone and continuing her set.

"Don't live in the past," she reminded herself as she was back on stage. Aimee Semple McPherson reinvented herself, and so would Mia, if necessary.

News Flash to the Past

"According to the AP, Aimee Semple McPherson disappeared on May 18, 1926 in the lovely seaside community of Venice Beach in sunny Southern California, just west of the magical town of Hollywood. There is a complete search for the body being made by lifeguards and the Search and Rescue teams off of the California coast.

More information will be shared when it is received. For up to date news, tune into KFWB Hollywood, News Radio.

Mrs. McPherson's mother and daughter still have hope that she will be found, safe and sound. Our thoughts and prayers are with you Aimee, come home safely."

A bump in the road brought Mia back to her slow taxi ride along Sunset Boulevard. Pushing

Aimee Semple McPherson out of her head was very difficult.

"Could you make a left here?" she asked the driver.

"Where miss?"

"At Taix Restaurant, could you make a left? Yes, here," she said.

She remembered the new location, but the old locale down in the old French Quarter section of Downtown Los Angeles was full of pleasant memories. As a girl, she walked between her parents holding each of their hands on their way inside of the Champ d'Or Hotel where the old Taix was located. The comforting vegetable soup or ratatouille with warm, crusty bread had been a childhood favorite that carried into adulthood, and reminded her of the tureen of soup they shared after her father had died in his sleep.

"Of course, Miss," the driver replied.

"Could you drive around the lake please? A left here," she said.

When the cab drove down the short street, there was the monstrously large temple looking building. It was the Foursquare Church. In the backseat, Mia thought about Aimee as they drove passed the Foursquare Gospel Church on Glendale Boulevard across from Echo Park Lake. The beauty of Echo Park, the boathouse, and the bridge. All of these landmarks must have brought Aimee pleasure at their simplicity and beauty of nature. There was a part of her that understood there must have been some event that made Aimee do what she did. She felt as if she was a part of the sisterhood. No amount of Hollywood back lights or wardrobe changes would erase the wrong that had been done to Aimee by Los Angeles District Attorney Asa Keyes or the city itself. Aimee had been elevated to cult status, just like the Four Square Church. Now she was alone. They were both alone, decades apart. The story was there though. A significant event and the consequences, parallel to Mia.

"Back up to the Boulevard?" the driver asked.

"Yes, take me home," she said, after the circular tour she was once again looking at the Four Square.

Just like Aimee, no amount of wishing could erase the wrong done to Mia. Why had she agreed to go on that piano circuit? No one had ever heard of a local tour of the lower states for a pianist. Mia knew she would never perform at Carnegie Hall, but she knew that she did have talent. The seconds, minutes, hours, and days she spent learning and practicing piano would pay off, she thought. All of the struggles her mother had faced to pay for her piano lessons and now the thought of sitting at a piano bench terrified her. Where at once she was at home and in love the minute she got on the keys, now the stabbing feeling in her heart prevented her from touching the keys. She was no longer in love.

Oh Aimee, why did you come home? Because there was no other place. I'm just like you.

"Seven dollars, please," the voice casually announced.

The trip home had been short and sweet. A longer trip would have stirred up even more memories of the broken and left behind of Echo Park. It had always been a mystery to her, but now there was a different light, almost diaphanous on her trip up Glendale Boulevard. Coming home had only made her love the area more. The City of Angels was her one and only love.

"You can never go home again," wrote the famous writer Thomas Wolfe. His words were never so untrue, thought Mia. She took the Mark Cross overnight bag that she had traveled home with for her quick escape. Most of her clothes and costumes were in the trunk that would be arriving later.

After the driver opened her door and she exited, she felt the prevailing westerlies embrace her with their forgiving spirit and kind kisses. They were so different from the Santa Anas that when they rolled into Los Angeles brought a spike in crime and violence with their unpredictability and harsh devil winds.

The Yellow Cab started to barrel down the street, a survivor of a Post war relic.

All the California bungalows on the street with their front porches and narrow driveways looked like movie stars homes after her trek cross-country. Tiny shotgun houses. Second-rate motels off major highways. Howard Johnson motels making her feel nauseous at the memory of orange and turquoise. So many different rooms and beds, but she was finally where she wanted to be. She was finally controlling her own destiny. Mia walked up the pathway and checked the front door, which was predictably unlocked. She opened the door and walked into the front room.

"Mommy, I'm home!" Mia proclaimed with a sense of surrender as she closed the door behind her.

Aimee Semple McPherson was found wandering near Agua-Prieta five weeks after she disappeared from the beach. The piano tour was Mia's very own Agua-Prieta, as close to the Arizona/Mexico Border as she would ever travel, as far away from her home that she would ever travel from. Her own escape. Oh, Sister Aimee, she thought, I need the Power of Faith. And I need to find the story of my own life.

Before "The Story of My Life" sermon could
be preached, it was all over.

News Flash to the Past

---

*"On September 28, 1944, the Los Angeles Times
reported Aimee Semple McPherson died yesterday.
The Evangelist passed away in Oakland on one of
her typical "magic carpet" crusades of whirlwind
activity. She was found in bed by her son Rolf, who
said that, although unconscious, she was breathing
heavily when he entered her room in the Leamington
Hotel at 10:30 a.m. Two doctors and an Oakland
Fire Department Inhalator Squad worked in vain
to revive her. She was pronounced dead at 11:15
a.m."*

Upstairs Above the Vista Theater

"You lost again, Red. This is just not your lucky night," bellowed from upstairs above the coffee shop, followed by roaring laughter from a group of male voices.

"I'll be right back," Red said taking the last swig of his Brew 102, and the last drag off his Tiparillo. He twirled the paper ring around his pinky finger and walked out the door. As he descended the stairs and walked through the double glass doors, Dean Martin's "You're Nobody Till Somebody Loves You," was playing on the radio. It was currently a top ten hit on the radio of 1964.

"Oh, my feet are killing me!" That's not something you hear in a coffee shop, he thought to himself. His mother often complained of her hurt feet. She would sit next to him on the couch reading to him from a book of poetry as she rolled her ankles.

Red heard the words shouted out as he entered the near empty coffee shop on the corner of Sunset Boulevard and Hillhurst Avenue.

"Sit anywhere," said the same voice, only sweeter and less angry. He hadn't heard such an honestly emotional voice since his mother years ago. The voice was not distinct when she spoke. He wasn't familiar with the voice and he was very familiar with many ladies in Los Angeles.

"Thanks," he mumbled as he sat in a nearby booth.

A menu plopped in front of him and still no face to match to the voice.

"You want coffee?" the voice yelled from across the floor of the coffee shop.

"Oh yes please, darling," he replied in the direction of the voice. A cup of coffee and a quick bite he thought would put him back in the winning seat. Or at least get him out of the losing seat. He had lost the last five games. Poker was never an exact science. The thought of getting another winning hand was what had pushed him to walk down the stairs — almost falling out onto nearby empty Sunset Boulevard. That and the thought of some female company. Playing with the boys was fine, but loving the ladies was his talent.

"Did you decide? Will it be breakfast?" Mia asked in a rush.

The side work that she was responsible for lay across the back table. One five-pound bag of sugar, and two coffee cans full of salt and pepper with a homemade spout for pouring in each can. Then a bag of cloth napkins she needed to fold for the morning rush. Side work completed before the shift was Mia's way, then she could go home and practice the piano.

"Oh hello," said the guy. "It's been a while."

He seemed to know her, but she had no recollection of him. Was he a customer? She had only been working here six months, so perhaps she reminded him of another waitress.

"Hello, sugar," replied Mia. She knew from experience to lead the guy on if she wanted a decent tip. Then she looked at the guy. Those piercing blue eyes and she knew it was Red.

"It's good to see you again. Could I get bacon and scrambled eggs with rye toast? Please, no whipped butter. I want the hard patties of butter if you don't mind," he completed his breakfast order like a laundry list.

"Good to see you as well," Mia replied. She recognized Red and remembered "Sway," and the awkwardness of their introduction. She hadn't seen him since she was at Blessed Sacrament. Red had no doubt of who she was and ten years later he was still intrigued. She noticed he was still good looking and she was caught up in the memories of the past.

During the graduation from St. Francis, Red listened to his brother Michael give his speech about the future. He was home for a visit and enjoyed the peace of the church and his brother's wise words. He listened to Michael speak about the responsibilities the graduates all had when they moved onto high school. He noticed a girl in the back row of graduates; a girl he did not recognize. From the back of her head, she looked beautiful. There was an undeniable quality about her, and it was not just her obvious beauty. From her seat, she looked like she was wearing a simple pink dress. He guessed there would be white lace trimmed socks with her black and white saddle shoes, typical for a teenager. After the World War II, it was commonplace to see young women in uniforms of all types of military, but the simplicity of the pink dress reminded him of his mother and how she loved the simple color of pink. But there was something different about this girl. Her dark brown hair was parted on the side like Veronica Lake. She had fine features. She was beautiful. Getting lost in the stranger made Red lose track of the mass and not kneel when it was time. He awkwardly remained standing and when he woke up from his trance, the entire church congregation was kneeling except him. Quickly, he self-corrected. Mia's friend, Jane, saw Red's attention and she poked Mia in the ribs and the two of them quietly giggled.

Trying to focus on the mass proved difficult for him as the object of his fascination turned around in his direction. Father Michael flashed a frown in Mia's direction and Jane squealed when she saw the look land at her friend. Red felt distracted. These young women of fourteen were graduating from eighth grade and then going to Immaculate Heart High School, cocooned in the simple high school of studies and prayer. There were no boys there; perhaps that was better for them.

Because Red was so inattentive in church, he prayed the mass would end quickly. He was shipping out for his tour and an uncertain future. Latin usually helped calm the thoughts and chatter in his head. But now the Latin ran together as his head spun and he felt warm in the coolness of the church. His mind hopscotched around what stuck in his head — the uniform, defending the nation and freedoms of the world. Red numbered the last parts of the mass to calm his speeding mind and body, especially his heart.

By numbering the parts of the mass, Michael had taught Frederick the parts of the ceremony. Ever since he was six, Michael had always known he wanted to be a priest. Frederick was not that lucky. After the death of their mother to cancer, Frederick had great difficulties concentrating. Frederick liked the ladies but did not want to get married, settle down and have a family. He wanted to see the world, and that was what the Navy would do for him. Michael Sr., Red's father, had no answers for all the girls who would come to the house to ask when Red was going to settle down. Red had no type. He loved all the ladies and they definitely loved him. Numbering the parts of the mass cleared a space in his head and brought order to his thoughts.

1. *Communion ...*
2. *Post communion ...*
3. *Concluding Rite …*
4. *Dismissal ...*

Mia kept her head bowed as Father Michael walked down the center aisle. By the time she looked up, the stranger walked past her on the center aisle. Mia stayed in the church for a moment saying three Hail Mary's and two Our Father's, an additional penance for her venial sins.

As she exited the church, she saw the uniform again. He was standing next to Father Michael. He was someone new. Father Michael motioned for her to join them. She felt nervous and warm at the same time.

"Mia, come over here and meet my brother, Freddy. He likes to be called Red, but he'll always be Freddy to me."

Mia walked over and was face to face with the uniform. As she looked into his face, with the same eyelashes and bluest eyes as Father Michael, he took her hand and kissed it with delicate, soft lips.

"Pleased to meet you, Mia. Cara Mia," he said smoothly. Then he twirled her in a Hollywood moment.

"Nice to meet you, Red," replied Mia, coming out of his twirl somewhat breathless.

In her imagination filled with 1940's and 1950's romantic comedies and musicals, her young mind wandered into a dream trance. In her head, they started a dance routine. A car on the street was playing Dean Martin singing "Sway" on the radio. Mia recognized the words and her mind took her to a Hollywood movie set, where she and Red were the stars. He held her hand and pulled her toward him. She could feel his warm, sweet breath on her cheek. Then he leaned over and whispered into her ear and she knew the words were meant only for her. He twirled her around like in the movies and then the two of them took bows for their imaginary dance. Mia's imagination was always active when she was near music. And she had a habit of mixing up the words and changing them up. Mia was great at filling in the words to others' music. Creating her own music was where she failed.

> *"When my heartbeat rhythms play*
> *Da da da, make me stay*
> *Hold me close, da da da*
> *When we dance, let's fly away."*

When Red was introduced to her and called her "Cara Mia," his mind wandered off to what a first kiss with Mia would be like. In his dream, he heard a car passing by outside of the church with Dean Martin singing "Sway" floating out of the window. He would sing words from "Sway" in an attempt to win her heart, because this was his standard pattern to win the hearts, minds, and bodies of the Los Angeles ladies. In this dream, he was so close to her ear she would feel his lips as he whispered the last words. Then he would twirl and hug her for a moment longer than he should.

He dated women who were older and more experienced. Women who weren't looking to give up their studio jobs and get married. She was still a fourteen-year-old school girl finishing off the eighth grade and about to start high school while he was a young man just turned twenty in the Navy ready to begin his first tour. But her innocent natural beauty touched his heart. Her sweet warmth reminded him of his mother when she would dance with him before she was sick.

Mia had a natural fit in his arms when he twirled her, Hollywood style. Perhaps this was why Michael told him to stay away from a girl in his parish named Mia. Michael said she was too young for him. She was pure. Red noted to himself Michael was correct. Mia was young and innocent. If he were to stay in Los Angeles, perhaps he would have more thoughts of her. For a moment twirling this incoming freshman in his arms, made him forget about his upcoming adventures on the high seas and defending our nation. Red had interacted more than he should have done with Mia.

On the steps of this beautiful church, it all seemed so different. Mia was caught up in her fantasy while Red was wrapped up in his own. Each of them heard the beauty of the words of Dean Martin singing "Sway" in the distance. There was nothing creepy about their obvious attraction. Michael knew it. Jane saw it and understood it, because she had seen it in the movies.

Father Michael watched them, he saw it out of the corner of his eye. Their greeting and introduction, and Red twirling her like she was a ballerina in a little girl's jewelry box. He always watched his younger brother's deep and wide appreciation of women. Father Michael rarely spoke to Mia after that day. She heard he was transferred to another church and his brother had completed his two tours of duty and came back to Los Angeles. But that was years ago, and she was different now, she was a full-grown woman capable of bad choices.

She remembered him, his closeness. The two of them had shared a moment, but each had a different memory of that moment. As it often does, life got in the way. Mia always wanted a creative life of success and performance. She graduated high school and went on a piano tour. Unfortunately, she didn't need her so-called manager's aggression in that hotel room. Finally, Mia returned home to her true passion, her baby grand. It was all she needed. Strange how life got in the way again.

"Who is that guy?" asked Johnny the cook.

"Someone I met years ago!" she snapped.

"He seems to know you. Did you go out with him in Florida?" Johnny asked. "I thought I was your one and only."

"Really, Johnny. What would your wife and three children say? Don't worry about this guy," Mia snapped.

"Order up," Johnny said as he rang the dish out bell.

"Did you butter the toast?" asked Mia.

"No, want me to?" he asked.

"No, he wants hard butter for the toast. I'll do it," she said taking the toast plate and putting it down. She buttered the rye toast, each top side and put it back on the plate.

"Here you go," Mia said to her customer.

"Looks great. Thanks. I'm down here looking for some new luck. I've lost a bundle upstairs tonight. Do you play cards, Mia?" he asked.

"Oh, I'm not a gambler," Mia stated. "Do you need anything else?"

"Can you sit with me?" he asked. "I haven't seen you in years. Last time I saw you Michael was still at St. Francis. That was a long time ago, when you were a young girl. We were both so young!"

She paused when he said her name; she was not used to this man letting her name fall so freely from his oh so perfect mouth. Now Mia was so removed from that young girl outside the church steps. She knew she would never, could never, go back to that naiveté. The pure belief and love of

God and his strength and protection. No God would allow the evil that had happened.

"I have a minute," she replied, as she sat in the booth opposite Red.

"Finally, a winning hand," Red thought.

Snapshot
Wedding Announcement

The Los Angeles Herald Examiner read:

"Frederick Crocetti and Mia Sullivan were married on August 5, 1961 in the rectory of St. Francis of Assisi by Mr. Crocetti's brother, Father Michael Crocetti. Mrs. Sullivan, mother of the bride, and Father Michael were the witnesses in attendance. The bride and groom honeymooned in Waikiki, Hawaii."

Snapshot
Birth Announcment #1

Just
Arrived

Baby Girl Crocetti
February 14, 1962
to
Mr. and Mrs. Frederick
Crocetti

Snapshot
Birth Announcment #2

Just Arrived

Grace Sharon Crocetti
November 18, 1965
to
Mr. and Mrs. Frederick
Crocetti

Snapshot
On the Front Porch

We are getting ready to go to church today. Uncle Mike is back in town. Daddy is putting on his tie and Momma has on a white suit with a large scarf over her head. In our Sunday best dresses, Gracie and I are trying not to get dirty. It is easier said than done because they dressed us in car coats and patent leather Mary Jane's. Daddy comes out to sit with us because Momma is not quite ready. Daddy said beauty takes time and patience. He sat with us on the front porch swing as a car radio blasted their song. Momma had perfect timing and as she walked through the door, Daddy held his hand out to her as the words were being sung.

"Da da da da da da

Hold me close, sway me more."

Then Daddy did the unthinkable, he held his hand out for me and I took it, and then he held out a hand for Gracie and she took it as well. The four of us danced that Sunday afternoon as my father sang the words beautifully among the captive audience of morning glories and his ladies. And I understood why Momma loved him so, because I loved him, and Gracie loved him too.

"When we dance you have a way with me
Stay with me, sway with me."

We were all so happy as we drove down to Blessed Sacrament to hear Uncle Mike say the mass. My wish was that it could last forever. I always wished for the good times to last forever like whenever I blew out birthday candles or dandelions. Unfortunately, wishes don't always come true. After a dinner of chicken cacciatore and a bottle of Chianti at Emilio's on Melrose, Daddy was not so sweet. Uncle Mike drove us home with Momma in the front seat and Daddy between us girls in the backseat.

The Wish Book

FADE IN:

EXT. HOUSE IN HOLLYWOOD HILLS — DAY

The large, white craftsman house sits in the Hollywood Hills far above the Boulevard, like a perfect beacon on the dead-end street. There is a large redwood gate and a tall flowering pittosporum tree and no sidewalk. Outside the house is a front porch, two great picture windows painted dark green, and a very handsome front door painted the same green fusion Japanese style with four narrow beveled windows. There is an old screen door made of hardwood with a ripped screen, it slaps against its frame and makes a cha-cha-cha noise. There are neighbors to the right, to the left, and above the house built in front of an old plank wood retaining wall. A rubber tree grows to the right of the garage in the neighbor's front yard, the leaves fall freely into the driveway.

DISSOLVE TO:

INT. BEDROOM — EVENING

Notes from a piano drift through the screen door which softly echo across the summer evening. ANNIE and GRACIE, two young girls sit in a bedroom on the opposite side of the house. They are quite young. Gracie is seven with Nordic blonde hair and hazel eyes. Annie is ten with dark brown hair and eyes. They are dressed in tie-dyed t-shirts and blue jean cutoffs. The younger girl is narrow and slim; the older girl has a chubbiness which she will outgrow with six more inches of height.

"I want to be just like you when I get older, Annie," the younger girl said.

"We're already alike, stupid, because we're sisters."

"But I want to wear braces like you. Look what I drew, look, LOOK!"

"Gracie, that's OK. Mine is better."

"That's 'cause you're older. When is Mom going to finish with Norman anyway? I hate having

31

to stay on this side. I can't have my garage sale," Gracie whined.

"That's stupid, Gracie. The only customer to sell anything to in the front room would be Mom and maybe Norman."

"You're right."

"This is boring. Let's look at the book again. The BOOK! THE BOOK! Don't worry, she won't catch us. I want to see all the pretty pictures and matching clothes."

"Gracie, let's put this stuff away first, so we don't have to do it later."

"No! I want the big book now. NOW! NOW! NOW!" Gracie screamed jumping up and down.

"You're such a stupid brat."

"Yeah, but you love me. You have to 'cause I'm your sister. Get the book. Please. Pretty please with maple sugar on it."

"Fine Gracie, but we'll have to pick up this stuff later," Annie said. She stood up and walked over to the bed. She pulled the Sears catalog out from under the bed. The wrapper is kept on it, it looks brand new, but it is last season's.

"Yeah! Yeah! You're such a great sis, Annie. Oh, look, I want this and this. Don't turn the pages so fast. Slow down, please Annie, slow down."

"I want the chubby girl's section." Annie delicately turns each page without leaving fingerprint patterns embedded on the pages.

"Why aren't there more pages for the chubby girls, Annie?"

"Don't you remember what happened last week, Gracie? Remember."

"No. What, Annie?"

"Well, when I called up the Sears lady she was real nice to me at first. Then I asked her why there weren't more clothes for big girls?"

"What did she say, Annie?"

"Gracie, she told me to lose weight." Annie says this with a tear in her eye. Gracie puts her arm around Annie and gives her a half-hug.

"It's OK, Annie, she was just a meanie. I still meant what I said. I want to be just like you when I grow up."

"No, you don't, Gracie."

"Wow, look at page 363. I love that. Let me go show Mom."

"Forget it. She has a lesson with Norman right now. She'll get mad and we'll never go out to the Ontre Cafeteria. And I am so hungry, so very hungry, Gracie."

"I still want to be just like you, Annie. Remember last year when you ran away. It was so great. You came back with that lip potion that all the girls on the Boulevard have. That was so great, Annie."

"No, it wasn't great, Gracie. It wasn't much fun at all."

Annie remembered the day with a fury. She had asked her mother for fifty dollars to buy everything she had wanted in the Sears' Wish Book. Her mother had said no. Annie walked out of the house and down the street. She walked down to the Boulevard.

DISSOLVE TO:

EXT. HOLLYWOOD BOULEVARD — DAY

Annie walked past the counter at Lee Drugs. She walked past the boy walking the bird puppet with the funny nose outside the arts and crafts gallery. She walked past the bikers outside Penny Lane.

INT. SWENSEN'S ICE CREAM PARLOR — DAY

She walked into Swensen's and ordered her favorite ice cream. Bubble gum ice cream with jimmies on top in a paper cup please. A mustached man sat next to her as she religiously ate a spoon of ice cream, sucked off all the ice cream from the gumballs, and then placed them on the

34

napkin in front of her. The colors bled into the white napkin. Blue. Pink. Yellow. Green.

"Hey gorgeous."

As he talked to her, he kept telling her how pretty she was. Hopes and dreams. Words and promises. He wanted to buy her dinner, but she was not hungry. He said he would take her to the movies, but first he wanted to go get a pack of gum.

EXT. HOLLYWOOD BOULEVARD
JJ NEWBERRY'S — DAY

The business of Hollywood was apparent by the groups of tourists and tour busses. They walked to Newberry's. He tickled the fingers on her hand with his fingers. It felt good to have a new friend that was so nice. He kept telling her how special she was.

"Hey gorgeous, I'm Ken."

When he said his name, Annie immediately looked up at him.

"My name is Barbie," she said and held her hand out like a princess to be kissed.

"Sweetie, do you want anything?" he said the words melting out of his mouth.

"I always wanted some lip potion, but my mother said I was too young." Annie picked up a package of the lip potion. It was bubble gum flavor, her favorite flavor.

"I bet that tastes real good," he said to her.

"This is great."

"We'll take this too," he said to the old woman behind the counter.

"Can we go to the movies now?"

"Sure, sweetie pie, anything you want." He held her hand and they walked back to the theater.

"Can we see 'Towering Inferno'?"

"Anything you want, sweetie pie."

"I really like you, you're real nice."

"I like you a lot too, Barbie. I think I'm gonna like you a whole lot more."

INT. LOBBY OF A MOVIE THEATER ON HOLLYWOOD BOULEVARD — DAY

"Yay. Yay. We're here."

"OK."

"Here we go. Why don't you go and pick us out a nice seat in the last row? After all, we want to see the big picture. I'll buy us some goodies."

INT. MOVIE THEATER ON HOLLYWOOD BOULEVARD — DAY

Annie walked into the dimly lit theater. She sat in the last row directly in the middle of the row. The theater was empty. As she made herself comfortable a couple walked past her. She took out her lip potion and put some more on. She liked the way it tasted. She liked the way it made her feel all grown-up. Annie wondered where her new friend was because the lights went out and the movie was about to begin. He came walking through the door with a large bucket of popcorn, Goobers, Raisinets, Red Vines, and a couple of sodas. The movie started.

"This is great, she said sipping her soda and eating popcorn. He had his arm around her chair. She watched the movie and he started to stroke her hair. She fidgeted in her chair.

"Is this all right if I do this, Barbie? You just tell me if you don't like it. But you are such a pretty, young thing, Barbie."

"It's OK," she said. There was no one around them. The couple had sat in the front row. She was thinking about Gracie, her mother and father.

"You're so pretty. Can I kiss you?" he reached over and kissed her on the mouth while grabbing at her undeveloped breasts.

Annie did not scream. She opened her mouth and nothing would come out. Annie turned around and looked at her new friend. She gave him the meanest look she had ever given anyone. Annie saw his right hand on her armrest. She grabbed his right pinky finger between her two small hands and pulled as hard as she could. Annie heard a pop, and then a whimper. She dropped his hand. Annie gave him the same hard look. He got up and walked out of the movie theater. Annie sat in the darkness of the theater with the candy, popcorn, and soda which had all taken on the flavor of bubble gum. After the movie ended, she sat for the next show, and then the next. She knew it would soon be dark outside.

A girl from the candy counter walked up to her and told her she would have to leave. Her body would not move. All she could do was hold her purse in one hand and the soda in the other. She was unable to speak, frozen in her chair. A little while later the girl returned with two policemen. One of them sat next to her.

"Are you OK, little one?" one of the officers said to her.

"I saw a guy with a mustache buy stuff and then come in here and sit next to her. He left more than a few hours ago. She hasn't even gotten up to use the bathroom," said the girl from the counter.

Annie could not speak. She opened her little purse and next to the empty wrapper from the lip potion was a card with her name and address on it. She handed it to the police officer who was sitting next to her. Annie had kept the wrapper because she was so excited about someone buying her something new and grown up.

"Come with us and we'll take you home," said the police officer with such a sweet voice.

Annie walked to the street and sat in the back of the dark car with the cage in it and no doorknobs in the back seat. Annie always thought the world was different from home life, but now she knew. Everything was the same. Unhappiness. Loudness. They drove street by street quietly *returning her to the house in the hills. As they arrived on her street, Gracie was standing outside waving at her. Annie waved back at her. The old woman who lives on the right side of the house looked out from behind her shades. The young couple who got stoned in the middle of the day outside by their living Christmas tree looked outside when they heard the police car. Annie got out of the car and Mia and Red ran out of the house and hugged her. Then they walked away and talked to the police officers.*

"Are you sure she's OK?"

This is all she hears. Gracie sees her and runs up to her and gives her a hug.

EXT. STREET OUTSIDE OF THE HOUSE — NIGHT

The police car drove down the street with its high beams and loud radio noises drowning out the songs of the crickets on this street that has no destination in the Hollywood Hills.

INT. RESUME BEDROOM — NIGHT

"I want to be just like you, Annie. You always do great things," Gracie said as she looked through the Wish Book.

"No, you don't, Gracie. No, you don't." Annie thought to herself, NO YOU DON'T! I won't let you do the things I did, Gracie.

I won't let you run away down to the Boulevard. I won't let you eat ice cream with jimmies on it and make a new friend. I won't let you go to the movies on your own. I won't let a new friend buy you bubble gum flavored lip potion. Annie says these things in her mind and knows in her heart she will save Gracie.

"I love you, Annie, I still want to be just like you. But next time you leave, take me with you. Promise, love you."

"I'm not going away anymore. And you won't either. We'll be OK. Now stop all your mush, OK stupid?" Annie laughed.

"I still want to be just like you, Annie, when I grow up. I also want to catch up with you in cookie sales."

"Both things will never happen, Gracie. Besides I'll always best you. I'm older."

"Love you, Gracie."

"Love you, Annie," Gracie said as she hugged her.

FADE OUT

Snapshot
He Only Had Eyes For Her

In the picture, Momma and Daddy are standing on either side of me. And I have an I'm-eating-cake grin on my face. We are all smiles. They are leaning into me. He with his full beard and moustache, she with her Lily Pulitzer pastel shift dress. For one tender moment, Momma is looking at me and Daddy has all eyes on her. And we are the American Dream. Daddy will love her forever, I can see it in his eyes. Momma has that pensive, focused look, like when you're trying to keep your eyes open and it is past midnight. She loves him for the moment. I think she feels that way about us girls too. Gracie doesn't see it because she is so young and needs Momma. Nana sees it. I see the way she looks at Momma sometimes, with a look of fascination and disgust. It's like after you rip the scab off, you still have to look at the open, festering wound and poke at it.

French Doors

Crash. The crazy yelling woke Annie out of her sleep. She sat up in her bed and saw the light on in the other bedroom. The light crept under the door. Annie looked over at Gracie's bed. It was empty. In the black of the night, she saw two eyes staring at her from the doorway of the noisy bedroom.

"How long have they been yelling at one another, Gracie?" Annie asked.

"Not shure."

"What's it about?"

"Can't shay."

"Are you OK, Gracie?"

"OK."

I look over at Annie and she knows I'm scared. I can never hide anything from her. She never lets me keep a secret. But my stupid lisp comes back when we have these nights.

"We'll be OK, Gracie."

"Uh-huh."

"I'll protect you, Gracie. I would never let him hurt you. Why don't you come over here and sit by me?"

"No, shis."

"Why not?"

"Cashse I'm not a little girl anymore, Annie."

"Yes, you are, and who cares anyway?"

"Daddy, he shays sho."

"Don't listen to Daddy, right now. He's not himself. And when did he tell you that anyway?"

Then I remember that I shouldn't have said anything to Annie. Daddy loves me and I know it. It was our little secret. Daddy took us shopping at Kinney Shoes and I got black patent leather Mary Janes. Then he took us to Sav-On for ice cream. I went out to the car and Annie was inside looking at some stupid magazine, Tiger Beat. Daddy was drinking from a bottle out of his glove box. He told me I could keep the secret of his soda pop, because I was a big girl now. On the long ride home, when we sang "Toot Toot Tootsie" and "Someone's in the Kitchen with Dinah," he winked at me from the corner of his eye. I knew it was because of our secret.

"I don't remember."

"Gracie, why don't you get into bed?"

"No."

"You're going to get into trouble."

"No, I won't. I'm a big girl now."

"If you get into bed, I'll tuck you in. And maybe I'll even pat you to sleep, the way Nana does."

"No, Annie. I don't want to."

The voices get louder and I am getting more scared. Pretty soon that Hollywood Division will be here. And then they'll put Daddy in the back seat of the car and take him away. And then Momma is in a bad mood. Nana comes over here and then they argue. And the whole house is mad.

The shadows under the door move quickly. I look at the shadows dancing in the light. I can't understand what they say; they are too loud and too fast. If the walls are so thin, why can't I hear the words?

"Gracie, if they find out you're up, you're in trouble."

"I don't care. I don't want them to take Daddy away again."

"Gracie, you don't know what you're talking about. He is in a bad mood. He's been in a bad mood a lot lately. They take him away and then he is better. He needs to dry out."

"Annie, what are you talking about? You want them to take Daddy away? How can you shay that?"

"It's better when he leaves."

"No, Annie. You're mean like Momma."

"Gracie, this isn't Daddy. When you think he is in a bad mood, he's not. It's all those drinks talking. And that 'soda pop' in the glove box. Please. Gracie, it's better when he leaves."

"No, I don't want to hear you."

Annie is just like Momma and I am just like Daddy. Momma snaps and Daddy takes it. Annie punches me and I take it. I put my hands over my ears so I don't have to listen to her.

"Don't you ever wonder what Daddy is doing with the rubbing alcohol in the backseat of the Falcon? It takes away the smell of beer."

"That's shtupid. Daddy likes clean handsh. He's always clean. He doesn't shmell."

"Dummy, you're such a dummy, Gracie."

"Shtop it!"

"You better get into bed, Gracie. If they find you up, you're in trouble."

The voices in the other room get really loud. They are louder because Momma and Dad are right behind the door. They don't make sense. I wish they would stop. Why can't they be normal? What's wrong with us?

The door hinge squeaks and the door opens. I hide behind the door. Momma walks into the room and goes over to my dresser. She opens the top drawer and takes our money jar. Momma does this to get rid of Daddy. It is all the money Annie and I saved. I look at her close the drawer. The light bothers my eyes as I see her walk back into their room. Daddy starts to yell again, and I watch him reach out both hands to take the jar as the door closes. Things are fuzzy until she closes the door and I can see clearly again.

"Did you see that, Annie?"

"Yeah, I did."

"Why didn't you shtop her, Annie?"

"I didn't want her to yell at me, or worse."

"Why'd sche do that, Annie?"

"She does it all the time, Gracie. You were just awake this time. She gives him money so he'll leave. Sometimes he gets out of here before the police show up. I'll make it up to you. We'll go down to the Boulevard tomorrow and collect cans. I'll bet we can find enough to go to Swensens and get ice cream."

"Annie, can I get bubble gum ice cream with jimmies on top?"

"Gracie, you can get any flavor you like. Whatever will make you happy."

"And you won't get sick if I do that gumball thing?"

"No, Gracie."

"I can't help it. I like to save the gum so I have something to chew as we walk the Boulevard.

Unless we stop on Yucca at the liquor store and get a big wad of Bazooka."

The front door slams. The beveled glass rattles. The house is quiet. I stand up and start to go to Momma's room. I walk over to Annie's bed. She lifts the covers and I climb in. She doesn't mind my cold hands and feet.

"Say your prayers, Gracie."

"I will if you take me to Grauman's Theater."

"All right, Gracie, all right."

"You know I love it there."

I love it at the Chinese Theater. I love to stand in other people's footprints. I pretend that I am someone else. I am a movie star and the world loves me. Everyone wants to hug and kiss me.

"Are you done yet, Gracie?"

"Not yet."

"Hurry up with your prayers, Gracie."

"Wait, I'm not done."

"What's taking you so long, Gracie?"

"OK, Annie, now I'm done. I prayed for all three."

"All three what, Gracie?"

"I pray for the people I know now."

"Yeah," said Annie.

"I pray for the people I knew before, the dead ones and their souls."

"That's good," said Annie.

"And I pray for all of the people I will meet, to protect them also."

"Oh."

"I want all to be happy and safe and protected by God."

"Gracie, did you pray for Daddy? Pray that they take him away. Pray that he stops drinking. Pray that he stops being angry at me and at you and at Momma. Pray that he stops scaring us."

"In Vacation Bible School they taught us about the devil and demons. I pray that Daddy gets rid of his demons."

"Gracie, in a lot of ways you are a big girl now. Now go to sleep. We'll wake up tomorrow to a brand-new day. We'll play in the sun. And when Daddy comes home, we'll run up to him and he'll swing us around and give us hugs and kisses and we'll pretend like nothing happened tonight."

"Promise, Annie."

"I promise. Now. OK, 'Now I lay me down to sleep. I pray the Lord my soul to keep. If I should die before I wake, I pray the Lord my soul to take.' Goodnight, Gracie."

"Goodnight, Annie. Sweet dreams."

Annie pats me to sleep. Outside our house I can hear the heaviness of the police car as it drives down our dead-end street. I can hear a woman's voice on the radio. I am glad they did not get Daddy. This time, anyway.

Snapshot
New York City

Momma and Daddy took us to the airport so we could go see Auntie Nan in New York City. This was our first trip to New York. I hoped we would visit the Plaza. When I was young, Eloise was my favorite girl in a book. She was always hanging around the Plaza having the wildest adventures. Since I got older, I like Pippi Longstockings books. They don't talk about parents. I like to escape into books when my parents start arguing. The funny thing is characters in books don't argue. They live perfect lives in the beauty of their paper lives.

"Why are they both driving us?" asked Gracie.

"I don't know," I whispered back.

"Well ask them," she said as she pounded into my arm like little baby socks.

"I'm not asking them anything," I replied.

Momma and Daddy were sitting in the front seat. There was not a bottle of rubbing alcohol to dilute the smell of his drinking in the backseat with a pile of newspapers. He would use the rubbing alcohol and newspapers to wipe all the smell out and clean his hands with the papers. My guess was that Daddy had not been drinking today. I forgot to check the glove box for a bottle because Momma was in the front seat next to him.

Together. Their heads were together. And he was singing in the car, his Rat Pack songs. Frank Sinatra. Sammy. Dean Martin was his favorite.

"Fly me to the moon and let me play among the stars," he sang as we took the long way of La Brea to the airport.

The last time we came out to LAX was to pick up Auntie Nan with all her boxes and baggage from the airport. I believed she was thinking of getting back together with her old boyfriend. She didn't even stay here a week. She was a freedom lover. Gracie will be a freedom lover as well. Me, I need to have people around me, since I don't have many friends now. When I get older I'm going to have friends and we're going to have fun like those girls at the Chateau Marmont. They walk through the lobby with their bandana halter tops and bell bottom jeans. Long, stringy hair passed their butts and the continual rolling of Lip Potion all over their post pubescent lips. I heard Momma describe Hanna and Sabra (my girl idols/crushes) like that once to Daddy. But I want lots and lots of friends.

Maybe the police can come to break up my parties instead of taking Daddy to jail.

Momma picked us up by herself from the airport two weeks later. She said nothing about Daddy. He wasn't at the house when we got home. I bought him a souvenir Statue of Liberty. I hope he likes it.

Apple Pie for Gracie

Our typical summer days were spent having fun. Gracie and I would spend the entire day down on the Boulevard. The cool granite so smooth against our small feet, the impressions of the stars centers scorching the underside. We would play pinball in the burger stand on the corner of Las Palmas. Looking out the tinted blue glass wall windows and hearing the Bay City Rollers singing on the jukebox, we would sit for hours watching. Girls with straight, stringy hair and ironed-on images of fried eggs on their chests danced with older boys. This was the first place I ever saw Hannah and Sabra. We were too young to be a part of their group, but they let us stay. If we were really lucky, they would let us go next door with them to the candy store.

I was baking with my green and white Suzie Homemaker oven, apple pie for Gracie. I opened the packets that were in the box. One packet was chopped apples, and the other packet was the dough mixture. I mixed them with water and preheated my oven to three hundred degrees. Gracie was playing with large, empty snail shells. She got them at a yard sale down the street in the apartments. Gracie hid them in her doll carriage and was examining them individually. She was wheeling the carriage around the front room, until Momma and Daddy began to argue. Then Gracie came to sit next to me. She always came to me when they argued.

Momma and Daddy argued. He smiled. My father kept smiling. I suppose he thought a smile would make her happy, like in the old days. It did not. She took Gracie's doll carriage and hit him over the head with it. As my father wore that carriage around his neck like a Hawaiian lei, he still had that smile on his face. That was his defense. He smiled.

After the police brought me home on the day I ran away, they always fought. I always tried to save Gracie. This is my sister job. I believed she was too young to get it. Was not. I got it. She thought life should be like "The Brady Bunch." We lived in a house with paper thin walls on a dead-end street high above the hopes and dreams.

They were never happy and I thought it was my fault. Momma was sadly in her own world. There were only two things she would do. She would sit at the piano and wave her piano fingers over the keys and play. She had a soft and gentle touch with the piano; it understood her. She touched that baby grand like I had never seen her touch us girls. Spoiling each key with love and pride oozing out of her fingertips, playing with an object that made her happy. She was happy. The only time she had any physical contact with us was when we got out of our baths. She would clean the potato bugs out of our ears. She would sit on the side of the old claw foot tub and have us put our heads in her lap on the towel. We would turn to the right and then to the left. She would lightly clean our ears with a q-tip, softly brushing the hair away from our ears. The only reason she did this was because Old Lady Johnson, the crazy lady down the street, wanted to know why we had ears as dirty as dogs.

Momma always seemed to be screaming at Daddy. She would run around with these wild, mad dog eyes. He looked at her and smiled. Her angry, red screams plagued our house. Often, I looked over at Gracie who seemed as if she were recording it all in her mind.

POW. She hit him over the head with Gracie's doll carriage. Her beloved pram. All the snail shells came tumbling out. Gracie screamed. Bits and pieces. He backed up into the wall and slid down to the floor while keeping his can of Brew 102 still upright. He fell asleep where he landed. Momma walked over to the piano and played a Judy Collins song. Gracie tugged on my shirt sleeve, my Suzie Homemaker oven was smoking.

"Tell Momma and Daddy!" screamed Gracie.

"They can't help us," I said as I glanced at the two of them in their own worlds. I opened the door to the oven, took out the apple pie with my pot holder, and threw it in the sink. I ran cold water and all of this smoke erupted. The water hit the apples and a gelatinous chunk hit my hand. As I looked at it, the bits melted onto my skin.

"Annie, rinse off your hand!" Gracie screamed.

"Ow!" I said in slow motion.

The skin was a shiny pink. As I touched my arm to feel the raised skin, there was a sharp pain.

"Are you OK?" asked Gracie.

"We'll be fine," I said.

The next day Daddy left with his MTM cognac leather duffle he got for Christmas and a brown paper bag filled with a six pack of Brew 102 and an opened bottle of Wild Turkey. Later in the day after Daddy left, Momma was in the kitchen crying at the table.

"Momma are you OK?" Gracie asked.

"Girls, why don't we bake?" She proclaimed wiping away the tears.

"Apple pie for Gracie!" I affirmed.

"We'll make it from scratch. We don't need any shortcuts in this life!" she asserted.

I watched Momma bring out the flour and eggs. She brought the basket of apples closer to her. She placed her measuring cups on the counter, lined up according to size. She lined up the ingredients according to their usage. Rows of unused appliances decorated the counters, freshly smelling from their boxes. She had begun her production. I stood by her as the assistant. Gracie sat on the counter singing "Itsy Bitsy Spider" with her stubby fingers in her own world. Momma and I cored Granny Smiths with new razor-sharp paring knives. The sun played hide and seek through the lace curtains in the kitchen. Gracie didn't notice that Daddy wasn't sitting in his green vinyl chair with a can of Brew 102 in one hand and beer nuts in the other. The details got past her. We saw Daddy on the weekends, but never again sitting in his chair with his can of Brew 102.

Gracie and I started to spend more time investigating the neighborhood. After all, Hollywood was the land of dreams and we could see all of the sex and drugs and rock and roll anytime we wanted to go down to the Boulevard and hang out with the other Boulevard brats. We didn't talk about that day...or many others that ended in fights, the police, singing in the bath tub or broken bones.

Snapshot
Hughes Market

Bean sprouts and those orange jelly candy slices with granulated sugar, those were my two snacks that I ate here when we came here to shop. Momma said, "We're just sampling to make sure everything is fresh and tasty." Some days I ate so much at Hughes, it ended up being my entire meal. Then I was not hungry. Momma made sure I got one of those paper-thin ham sandwiches with the crust cut off. But Momma still shopped here using her food stamps. Food stamps look like money, but she ripped them out of a paper book. I watched the old lady behind us scrunch up her face when my mom took the booklet out of her purse. Momma made sure we had dinner before she went off to play the piano for the night. One of those thin meat sammies, a glass of Tang, and Pik-Nik Shoestring Potatoes. She spread out a tablecloth on the floor in the front room and we picnicked there. Usually Momma does this after one of those nights when she didn't come home. It was OK. Momma said not to tell anyone. I fall asleep after the warm milk she gives to me. Annie told me she drank it once, but woke up with a terrible headache the next day. Annie said the sunlight felt like it was melting her eyelashes when she woke up. She said it felt like she was on Tilt-a-Whirl when she drank the milk. Now Annie stays up all night long. I know this because she told me so. She has dark patches under her eyes the next day. Momma love.

Snapshot
Divorce, California Style

Following the Russian Revolution of 1917, the Bolsheviks instituted the No-Fault divorce.

"The time has come to acknowledge that our present social and legal procedures for dealing with divorce are no longer adequate." — Governor Edmund G. Brown, Sr., 1966, explaining his support of No-Fault divorce reforms.

In 1969, California became the first state to permit No-Fault divorce when Governor Ronald Reagan signed it. The law went into effect in 1970.

Sacramento (UPI)-Gov. Ronald Reagan today signed the first major California divorce reform law in nearly a century that will make it easier and quicker to end an unhappy marriage.

"I believe it is a step towards removing the acrimony and bitterness between a couple that is harmful not only to their children but also to society as a whole," said Reagan, once divorced himself.

It becomes effective Jan. 1 but any divorce complaint filed this year that goes to trial in 1970 will also be subject to the new law.

On January 1, 1973, Mia Crocetti filed for a No-Fault divorce. It was the beginning of her own revolution.

The Big Man

Momma said we had to behave ourselves. We had to be nice and cross our legs at the ankles. Lady-like behavior and all of that charm school stuff. We had to be polite. I couldn't pull Gracie's hair until the tears welled up in her eyes. We didn't want to go. Gracie and I would rather sit at home and watch the new Mouseketeers on the television. Mom said we had to go and meet her new friend. I didn't want to meet him, I already knew what he smelled like. Sometimes when Mom came home late at night, I heard her humming in the bathroom. She sat on the side of the tub and took off her pantyhose and cocktail dress. Then she slipped on this old blue house dress with embroidered yarn flowers in pink and green. When she left the bathroom, I could smell this weird smell. The room smelled like dead animals.

She loaded us in the old blue Volvo and drove us down the hill. Gracie was excited. She pretended to be a dog and hung her head out the window. Sometimes I got embarrassed because she starts barking at people on the street. And she growled and whined. And Gracie wanted to meet this man. I have no interest in him. He served no purpose in my life.

We drove down the Boulevard, and then Momma made a right down Western Avenue. Mom parked in front of a tall building across from Builders Emporium and All-American Burger. There was a butcher shop, Monty's Meats. Above this shop was a hotel, the Gaylord Hotel. This man made my mother smell because he cuts up raw meat and has his hands filled with blood daily. My mother turned off the car engine and then looked in the mirror. She took her compact out of her purse and blotted her face. She took her Fire and Ice red lipstick out of her purse and reapplied it on her mouth. I watched her pucker in the mirror and blow kisses at her image.

"How do I look, girls?" she asked.

"Beautiful," Gracie screamed.

I ignored her. I heard about these men from Nana. She told me to watch out for them. I wished I wasn't here. I don't want to meet my mother's new boyfriend.

"Let's go girls."

"Go where, Momma?" I asked.

"Don't give me a hard time, Annie. Why can't you be more like your sister? Why can't you have all the enthusiasm that Gracie has? Give Gus a chance. Let's go in now."

"I'm not stupid. Go where?"

"Annie, don't be rude. Let's go, get out of the car."

We got out of the car and walked into the lobby of this hotel. The lobby was old and brown, and smelled of cigarette smoke. The place was greasy. There was a man standing behind a front desk counter reading "Playboy." He looked at the magazine, then at us, and then back to the magazine again. We walked down the hall. An old man sitting in a chair next to the elevator started to touch Gracie. My mother grabbed Gracie's hand and walked us up the staircase. I followed behind them. I could smell the filth as we walked up the creaky wooden stairs covered with vomit green carpet. The handrails were brown from dirty hands and nails that scratched it. I followed my mother and Gracie. Gracie held her hand as she counted each step she walked up. We walked up three flights of stairs, forty-five stairs to be exact. We paused outside room thirty-five. Mom straightened our dresses and fixed our hair by licking her hand and then she pushed it down. My hair was curly, so she kept trying to straighten it out without any luck.

Momma knocked on the door. I heard heavy footsteps walk to the door. I heard the deadbolt slide through the wall and the door opened. There was Gus. He was a big man. He was tall and bald and fat. I looked at this man and I looked at my mother. I could smell the dried blood as I looked at him.

"Hi, hun," my mother cooed at him as she kissed him on the lips.

"So, these are the girls."

"Yes, this is Gracie."

Gracie shook his hand silently, and then stood behind Mom.

"This must be Annie, hi," he said. He reached his hand out to me and I could see the dried blood under his fingernails.

"Hello," I said as I brushed the palm of his hand.

Gus breathed loudly and wheezed as he ushered us into his room. There was a kitchenette with a table and two chairs, and a living room with a burgundy corduroy sofa. A dusty exercise bench sat in front of the television, just another seat.

Gracie and I watched television all afternoon long. My mother and Gus sat at the table talking and drinking. He kept topping off the drink she had. They weren't even in another room; this place was so tiny. My mother didn't like us outside on the streets. She said below Sunset Boulevard down here by Western was busy and dangerous, so we would have to stay inside this apartment for hours. We watched television and did sit-ups on the exercise bench among the stacks of girlie magazines. And whenever we got out of line, as he said to my mother, he would take care of it.

Last Saturday afternoon we kept asking Mom when we could go eat because it was near dinnertime and we still hadn't had lunch.

"I'm hungry, Annie, really hungry."

"I know, Gracie, hang on. Mom, can we go eat?"

"Annie, ask again," insisted Gracie.

"Mom, it's been ten minutes. We're hungry. Can we go eat?"

"Mia, you have to learn to control your children. Don't let them control you. You are the parent. They will listen to you or else. Lay down the law."

"Gus, don't tell me how to raise my children."

"Mia, tell those children you are the boss."

Gracie and I listened to this exchange. Gus bent closer to my mother. I saw her touch the side of his face, and he kissed her on the cheek. I looked at Gracie.

"Annie, I'm so hungry."

"Mom, we need food. We're starving."

"Girls, don't talk that way to your mother."

"But Mom, we're hungry."

"What did I say to you, Annie? When we're ready to leave for dinner, we will."

"MOM."

"Stop it, Annie. Respect your elders," said Gus.

"You're nobody. You're not my father. You can't talk this way to me."

"Don't speak to me in that tone, Annie."

Gracie looked at me. Gus walked toward me. My mother sat at the kitchenette table.

"MOM!" I screamed.

Gus grabbed both of my wrists, squeezing. I saw the dried blood under his nails and the shadow of it on his skin. He smelled of the blood of innocent animals.

"Stop it, Gus!" I screamed louder.

"You have to learn to behave somehow."

I tried to kick him, but he stood too far away. I felt like a calf, attempting to run away from his fierce grip. I couldn't get my hands free.

"It hurts. MOM! Help me!"

My mother sat at the table reading her magazine, taking another sip from her drink and attempting to ignore this entire situation. Gracie began to cry. She was rocking back and forth on the couch, crying louder and louder, just like she did when Momma and Daddy argued in the front room at home.

"I can't concentrate!" my mother said. She stood up wobbly.

I kicked Gus so hard he let go of my wrists and I ran out the door. I sprinted down the three flights of stairs and passed the old man sitting at the elevator. He saw me and started to laugh with his toothless grin. The man at the front desk cackled as I ran out of the door and away from that stale air. I stood on the sidewalk by the car waiting for my mother and Gracie. I kicked the tires because I was so upset. I stood on the street crying. People looked at me as they walked by. Nobody offered me any help or consolation; I wasn't that type of girl. It seemed forever before my mother and Gracie came out of the hotel. My mother grabbed me by my right hand, opened the back door, and threw me in the backseat. I got a mouthful of the dirty blue vinyl upholstery.

"Why must you girls ruin everything?" my mother slurred as she slammed the car door shut.

The car was unbearably silent. I didn't say a word on the ride home. I missed my father terribly.

Snapshot
Camp Hollywoodland

"If you kill a moth and then rub your eyes, you'll go blind." That was the campfire tall tale the older girl told me in line for the sink at camp. I hated brushing my teeth, let alone brushing them in front of all of the girls here in camp. I'm only six, but Momma said I was seven. She told me to be a big girl and not to cry. There were times when being the baby of the family stinks. Going to camp was one of them. Usually, Momma kept me home while Annie went. Now I went with Annie, and we were in the same cabin.

"I need a break from you girls. You're driving me crazy," she constantly screamed out at us. Followed by the signature line she said daily, "This is crazy!"

KP duty. Apple butter. Campfires. Buying candy from the store. Calamine lotion. Walk on the paths. Lookout for snakes. Watch out for ticks. And then there was the constant smell of dirt, or dust, or pine needles. Just nature. Everything smelled of nature. But it was better to be away from the fighting. Always fights. The Police in their cars. Daddy getting a ride in the backseat. Gus visiting the house. Nana walking away. No more trips to Toy Loan. I miss those afternoons and the trip to the Golden Room. I always returned my toys in good shape for ten borrows and then I went to the Golden Room. A toy of my choice was the reward.

Snapshot
The Magic Shop

D oublemint finger snap was my favorite gum trick. But I've bought most of the tricks in this place. Stinky soap. Fly in the ice. Whoopee cushion. For some reason, I really liked to cause others pain. But I always stayed away from black soap. I knew that would make everyone angry at me, especially Nana.

The house was quiet these days. Annie laid in bed reading her Judy Blume books. I read the Nancy Drew books. Momma wrote words to other's music.

Auntie Nan moved to New York City. Auntie Bean doesn't invite us out ever since Uncle Steve died.

At Uncle Steve's funeral, his daughter, my girl cousin, told me that Red could have been her father. I was so shocked. I mean I thought my mom and dad were made for each other. They laughed and fought and hugged one another so much. Some mornings I walked into the dining room and they stopped talking at the table among their coffee and toast. I told my mom this and she laughed. She said she knew Red was the one when she saw him in his Navy uniform at the St. Francis Church when she was in the 8th grade.

Possum

It was siesta time, as I learned in school, and I was resting. I was on the rust and vanilla tapestry patterned sofa with large oversized arms watching the clouds play tag in the sky, watching through the lace curtains and large picture window. The clouds made the house light and dark, and it went back and forth.

Momma was in the kitchen. I heard her singing to the radio.

I really was asleep, when the doorbell rang. Mom answered the door after fixing her lips and running her fingers through her hair. She stashed the apron she was wearing by my feet; it almost made me laugh. Then I heard the door open.

"Cara Mia, my beloved," Daddy said with his customary flourish. It was like he was still on set, when he was a child actor, not an adult actor. The only reason he was a baby actor was because his mother was standing outside of the studios on Glendale Boulevard and the director needed a quiet baby for a scene.

I was laying on the sofa with my face pushed in to the corner of the cushions. I was trying to listen to Momma and Daddy talk. They thought I was asleep. I leaned toward the direction of the kitchen, with my eyes closed so tight I could feel my eye sockets. I wanted to see them, but they would not let me stay in the room when they were talking.

"Red, what do you want?"

"I bring presents."

"You shouldn't have come, Red."

"Can I come in, or do you have company?"

"Don't be foolish, the girls are here. Gracie is asleep on the couch right there. Come into the kitchen, we can close the door."

"I knew this was the right day, my lucky day. My fortune cookie said I would be rewarded if I shared the wealth, so that's what I did, my beloved."

"Come into the kitchen before you wake Gracie up. Have you been drinking? You smell of beer," she asked.

Then the door swung shut, and their voices were muffled under my blanket.

"Anything you say, my beloved."

Even with my eyes closed, I smelled the beer from Daddy. When the door swung shut, I caught a glimpse of Daddy carrying three boxes, one large and two smaller boxes. They were white and gold, with gold ribbon, boxes that looked like they were from The Broadway Hollywood.

Here I was playing possum on the sofa, so I could hear what they said. At Vacation Bible School last year at First Presbyterian, they said it was bad to listen to other people's conversations. But I was the youngest daughter and no one ever told me anything. I had to listen just to learn, and that's why I played possum. And besides, I was Catholic, so I didn't think they meant me. I only had to listen to the Pope.

"Why are you here, Red?"

"I brought presents for all of my beloveds. You and the girls."

"We don't need your presents."

"Cara Mia, give me another chance."

"Red, I don't want to get into this again."

The water was running in the kitchen. Momma was washing pots and pans. I could hear her harsh scrubbing with the steel wool. I could hear everything they said, because the walls of our house were paper thin.

"Paper thin walls, such a shame, paper thin walls," Nana said a long time ago.

I punched a wall once, when no one else was around, because I wanted to see if it would crumble. Paper, scissors, rock was how it went. But I got a bloody knuckle, the wall wasn't dented. In my closet there was still a drop of blood from my hit. The closets in this house always seem to hold secrets. When I was even younger, I would hide in the closet in my parents' bedroom amid the mess. I loved feeling the silky dresses and delicate lace on my mother's dresses. Sometimes I could hear them whispering sweet words and kisses. They were so nice to one another.

"Mia, I brought you a present. I know how much you love surprises."

"Red, I don't want anything from you."

"It's that big guy, the one the girls talked about, isn't it?"

"Move on, Red."

"Don't tell me what to do, Mia. You know I always hated that. We should stay together for the sake of the girls. They need a father figure in the house. Someone to protect them. And besides, we're married. In the eyes of the Church, we're married for life."

"Red, we weren't married in the Church. We were married in the rectory."

"Oh, my beloved. Do you forget so easily, Father Michael and his blessing of our union?"

"Red, I'm tired and it's almost time for dinner. Why are you here?"

"I told you my beloved, I bear gifts. Go get the girls and we can have Christmas in July."

"I told you the girls were busy. I'll let the girls open their presents later, after dinner. Please leave. I can smell the beer on you. Please just go."

"You open yours, my beloved."

"I don't want to, Red."

"Please, for me."

"If I open this Red, then will you leave?"

"We'll see if you want me to leave, Mia."

"I want you to leave, Red, really I do. I wanted to feed the girls dinner and let them do their homework, and go to bed."

"My beloved, here is your present."

I heard the quick unwrapping in the kitchen. In a fury, Momma ripped off the bow and opened it up.

"What is it, Red?"

"It's a fur coat, my beloved. Let's dance. Do you remember the first time I took you in my arms?

"It's synthetic. It's not real. That was a long time ago. We were both so young and inexperienced."

"But now we have experience to build on. It's a fake fur, Mia."

"So, it is."

"For a real fur, you'd have to give me a son. Now give me a proper thank you,"

"Thank you, Red. Now please leave."

"Come on, give me a kiss. Make me thrill as only you know how. Sway me smooth, sway me now."

"Leave now, Red."

"A kiss first."

"Leave, Red."

"Come on. Well then, I'll have to take it. I'm still your husband. Owwww!" said Red, as his voice seemed to travel toward the floor.

A large thud fell on the floor. It sounded heavier than the skillet I had seen dinner made in. The sound was heavy and unfamiliar.

"Get up and go home, Red. You're drunk. I asked you nicely. And now I'm going to ask you not so nicely. Do you want to meet my friend the cast iron skillet again?"

"No, I'm leaving. But let the girls open their presents before I leave." He said as his voice regained its strength.

"Here." She was helping him to his feet. "Red, they'll do it after dinner. Leave now, please."

"Anything you say, my beloved Mia. Mia Cara. But I'll be back. I'll be back in this house yet. I love you so."

My father walked past me and out the door. In my dreams, he would see me. He would sit next to me and smell like lilacs or the night blooming jasmine that grows up here in these hills. He would touch my face and wiggle my ears. And he would tell me that he loved me, even though we don't live under the same roof in this paper house anymore. This was my five second dream as I heard the door slam me back into reality.

We ate dinner silently. Burned hamburger patties. Succotash. Dried Pik-nik shoestring potatoes fresh out of the can. There was no dessert. Momma didn't believe in it.

I watched Momma shove the fake fur coat back in the box, she opened up the closet door and put it on the floor of the closet. She slammed the door shut behind her as if she was reminding herself of the decisions she made. There were so many secrets in the closets of this old house.

After dinner, I went to my room to open my present. Slowly, I unknotted the gold ribbon and saved it to make a bracelet that I could wear tomorrow in order to show off my present. I lifted the box top. I opened the tissue paper. For a second, I daydreamed that it was a possum because my Daddy knew me so well. But in reality, it was a Doll of the World they sell at the ARCO on Franklin. He must have had them wrapped at The Broadway Hollywood. But I already have this one, Miss Argentina. I put her back in the box and slid her under the bed.

Snapshot
Yamashiro

Sometimes Annie and I would sneak up to Yamashiro with Dee Dee. This old relic in Hollywood was filled with the pretty and fancy young from what we ever saw of the place. There was an apartment house and a restaurant. Although the apartments were empty like a ghost town, we knew that people lived in all of them since the mailboxes were filled with names of the renters. When we skated up there, no one scared us off.

This beautiful palace-like restaurant was built as a hilltop mansion 250 feet above the Boulevard. Dee Dee bragged that she had been in the bar with Wendy and some other friends of her mother's. Old man friends. But we just rolled. Rolled on our boards and when we were too lazy to carry them rolled down the grass. We rolled down the main lawn past the severely manicured bonsai. One of the gardeners told me that each cut had to help the appearance and the health of the tree. But they looked like mini-trees to me — one's that could be outside my Barbie doll house. Barbie and Ken could be happy with a bonsai in the front yard of their Dream House. We had a tree in our front yard, a blooming pittosporum. Sometimes Momma went out there and cut the lowest branches, but she couldn't reach the top branches. They were just out of her reach.

Beyond the fence, I heard some ladies' voices laughing at my mom's swinging hacks at the tree. They said she should probably check the roots for decay and leave the flowers alone. I wondered if those were the women who sent my mom a letter telling her she was doing a bad job raising us girls. They told her with words that she was a bad mother.

I stood by my mom who was crying as she struck out at the tree branch. In the crack of the gate, I saw Dee Dee in the backseat of the convertible Cadillac driving down the street with Wendy in the front seat and Norman driving the car. People to see and places to go on a Sunday afternoon.

Snapshot
The Scented Gift Garden

Nag Champra was the incense that they light and sell at this head shop on the Boulevard. I liked the smell of the incense and the velvet posters with their wild fluorescent colors. Women in iron bikinis. Tigers in tall grass on a savannah. Even Raggedy Ann and Raggedy Andy made an appearance, one sitting on top of the other. I don't pay attention to the pipes, paper or bongs. Gracie can't come in here because she would embarrass me with her baby lisp and unanswerable questions.

The lights were low and it was easy to get lost in this shop next to the Herman Munster House on the Boulevard. The first time I came in here I was following Sabra and Hannah. I overheard them talking about a place called Maclaren. It sounded fun. There were no parents and you slept in bunk beds in cabins. School was right there so they didn't have to walk anywhere. It sounded better than Camp Hollywoodland.

Those girls were cool. Long hair bleached by the sun. Puka shell necklaces around their tanned necks. A bandanna halter top, and a Hang Ten striped t-shirt. cut-off jean shorts, and flip flops was their California girl style. The halters barely covered their belly buttons and they seemed so at ease with their bodies.

I was supposed to be home over an hour ago and Nana was going to be so mad at me. But on my wish list for Christmas was one of those Hang Ten t-shirts with the little feet on the left-hand side, striped or solid, it made no difference.

Hollyhock House

E ver since Annie ran away, she liked to know where I was all of the time. We had to do everything together. She even signed up for the same art classes that I did. I looked around at the other kids at our table, and they didn't have shadows. They got to be all alone in the class, unlike me. The Spanish girl wore dark braids that ran down the length of her back and she was alone. The Japanese boy wore thick, coke bottle glasses and breathed loudly when his mouth was closed and was solo as well. The brown-haired girl with dancing green eyes and narrow fingers who laughed like a grown up and flirted with the teacher as she kept pulling up her bubble top never had a shadow. There were other kids, but they didn't sit with us. Annie sat on the grey stool, right next to me.

"What are you making?" Annie asked.

"A bird," I answered.

"What kind of bird?"

"A bird," I repeated brat-like.

"I'm making a dove, the international sign of peace. Come on Gracie, just tell me," she pleaded.

"Quit buggin' me," I snapped. I watched her as her shoulders wilted. She wasn't used to me snapping at her.

"Fine," Annie responded. "Last time I ask you anything."

"I'll be right back. I'm gonna get a drink of water," I said.

"Wait a minute, I'll take you," she said her hands full of plaster of Paris and cloth strips.

"I'll be fine," I said and walked out of the door.

As I walked to the drinking fountain, the lawn mower rumbled across the grass. Grass blades littered the lawn like confetti at a bon voyage party. The sunshine at Barnsdall was transparent. I stood with my arms stretched out and my face soaking in the rays of the great sun god. A paper plate blew to my feet and I ignored it. I stretched my small hand down and pulled out a dandelion. As I held it in both hands and brought it up to my mouth, I blew hard. All the spores blew away with my wish. The blush of color from the paper plate brushed up against my feet again.

In front of the Hollyhock House, there was a woman sitting cross legged. I walked up to her. The woman had chocolate brown hair pulled up high on her head and pink blush that sat in circles in the middle of her cheeks. She looked like a Raggedy Ann doll. Markers were fanned out in front of this woman. When the glitter jars were opened, metallic specks spilled onto the concrete. If front of the woman were paper plates, dozens of paper plates. As I walked up to the woman, I could see designs on the plates. The woman was drawing a silhouette on a plate with a thin black marker. She finished and put the plate back down on the ground.

I stood over her, staring at her creations. The psychedelic colors were bright and cartoon-like. Plastic turquoise and orange. Paisley. It was the bright yellow which covered the smiling face trash can at home. Thick round lines. Fine dashes. Dots. Wispy strokes. Shaking glitter pots like salt and pepper shakers on a dinner table. Things that were drawn becoming life-like through her Stabilo markers. Art imitating life, and vice versa.

"Hi," I said.

"Hello," said the plate lady.

"I like your plates. They're pretty. Look at all of the colors, like a rainbow or color wheel," I said gracefully leading my hands across the plates to display my intention like they showed us to in charm school.

"What's your name?" asked the plate lady, her face fixed on her drawing and not looking up at me. She had such concentration at every small masterpiece.

"My name is Gracie," I said.

"That's a pretty name for a pretty little girl," she said.

"Thank you," I replied. "I'm making a bird for the Christmas tree. It won't look as good as these, but I'm trying."

"All you can do is try. My plates don't always come out the way I'd like them to. That's the life of an artist. But I do my art on paper plates, because I can always throw them away if I don't like it," said the lady.

"Paper plates are throw away stuff. I've only used paper plates at parties and picnics. We don't use paper plates at home," I admitted.

"It's a disposable society. It's easier to throw things away rather than fix them," she said.

"GRACIE! Come here!" Annie screamed across the courtyard.

I waved for her to come over to where I was. I watched her run to me with a look of both terror and anger on her face.

"I'm talking to the plate lady," I said pointing at the lady.

"We have to get back to class!" She demanded.

"Why don't the two of you pick out a plate. Any plate you want, and you can have it, free of charge," said the lady.

"I don't want anything from some crazy lady," responded Annie.

"I do," I said.

I walked up and down the rows of plates. There were so many different colors and designs. When the sun hit the glitter, they all looked magical, pixie dust and fairy tales.

"I like this one," I said.

"That's my favorite," said the plate lady. "May it bring you all of the magical happiness it has brought me to create."

"It's all nonsense," said Annie. "She's just a junky old lady in a park bothering little kids. Get out of here old woman, before I call the police."

"Don't say that," I said.

I looked at the plate lady's face and her smile was gone.

"Let's go," demanded Annie.

"Bye, Gracie," said the plate lady disturbed.

"Bye," I replied.

Annie was silent as she grabbed my hand and dragged me back to the classroom. She finished her dove and they hung it at eye level on the magnificent Christmas tree in the entrance at Barnsdall Gallery. I made a quail with round antlers and a huge body. It rested at the bottom of the tree because it was too heavy to hang. It was magical with all the colors of the rainbow and glitter sparkling against the pure white lights on the tree.

I never saw paper plates blowing in the wind again outside of the Gallery up at Barnsdall or outside of Hollyhock House. One time I thought I saw the plate lady at Santa Monica Beach when I was twirling on the rings, but they were just empty paper plates in the wind.

Snapshot
Swensen's

Pink bubble gum ice cream with jimmies on it! That's how I did it every day if I could. Annie only ate chocolate. With all the flavors they made here in this factory, she only ate chocolate.

When she was in a good mood, we sat on the window side of the Boulevard. I looked at all of the boys across the street at The Gold Cup. The neon lights on the sign making the cup of coffee have burned out and the coffee cup has no steam rising from it. The only lady I saw in the place was the waitress. I never understood why there were only boys and men eating at The Golden Cup. But the GC was painted an ugly golden yellow and I had no love of that gold. Although the neon cup of coffee looked good. I would drink it like Momma, double cream and double sugar.

"Hey, stop kicking me," I screamed at Annie who brought me out of my snapshot.

"Sure, Dumbo," she said kicking me again, but then kissing the top of my head.

Annie and me. Me and Annie. Sisterhood forever.

Iggy, the Book, and the Lie

I hated the red plaid jumper with the white blouse and peter pan collar they made me wear to school. And those stupid saddle shoes I wore, black and white with clay bottoms. Annie likes her uniform because she gets to wear a blue plaid skirt and white blouse with square collar. I wanted to go back to Selma Avenue Elementary where I could wear whatever I wanted. That was where all of my friends were. Dee Dee, my best friend went there. I had my classroom at the YMCA down the street on Hudson, because the school was so overcrowded. I spent third and fourth grade watching men walk around the Spanish tiled courtyard on their way to the pool or weight room. I stared out at the courtyard and watched them. Sometimes when they caught me looking at them, they would smile back. One time I saw a young man standing with his back against our French windowed doors. He wore tight blue jeans and his t-shirt was skin tight. I saw the outline of the muscles in his back. When he turned around, I saw Raggedy Ann and Raggedy Andy on his shirt. Raggedy Andy was on top of her. I turned back around to see what Mrs. Jefferson what talking about. I didn't look out the window after that.

Dee Dee wasn't in my class at Selma. She was in the gifted class. The day they sent home a notice to my mother about testing me for gifted, she laughed. But she signed the note. I spent a whole afternoon in a windowless bungalow with a small, ugly man putting cubes into boxes, making the patterns with the boxes look like pictures he held up and talking to him. That was back in June, when school was ending.

In September, I was enrolled in Blessed Sacrament School, an old school with dark hallways and no heat. I was always cold. I hated this school filled with boys and girls who never talked to me. They had been going here since the first grade and I was new. Our teacher was new, but I hated her as well. Sister Marie Jean was her name. So much homework. I carried home a book bag full of books and hours of homework. Selma was never this hard.

Dee Dee and I didn't hang around anymore. She had our Selma friends and I had none. The kids in my class ignored me. I didn't talk to the kids; I didn't need them.

Every day at lunch, I created my own ceremony. I took the dollar Momma gave me and I bought two-day-old glazed doughnuts and milk, and I sat on a purple bench facing the Boulevard. I ate my lunch all by myself, because I didn't need anyone. Everyday a small nun walked by me on her way to noon mass. She smiled at me and said hello. That was the one act of kindness I experienced daily. My mouth was usually filled with doughnuts, but I mumbled hello.

She walked in small steps and kept her hands in her pockets. I looked forward to her walking by me because she said hello and didn't ignore me purposely. Her habit was floor length with small serious shoes peering out. She had a silver pin, a heart with thorns around it. The pin was very old and smooth from wear. She didn't wear the new habit like Sister Marie Jean, who showed her calves and had a short veil on her head.

Today I sat on my purple bench and ate my doughnuts. I could see my sister Annie playing tether-ball across the schoolyard. She was the champion. We couldn't socialize; she was in the eighth grade. I saw the nun walking from the convent. I swallowed my doughnut, so I could say hello. The nun walked up to me. She stopped. I could feel the thick black material against my leg as she sat next to me. She starred in the direction of Hollywood Boulevard alongside me.

I turned to look at her and she looked at me. She was quite old, way older than Nana. Her wrinkled pink skin and sky-blue eyes stared at me. She was nicer than Nana.

"Little one, why aren't you playing with the other children?"

"Sister, they don't like me."

"Nonsense," she said as she touched my hair like my mother does.

"It's true."

"Every day I see you on this bench as I go to noon mass. You always look like you are daydreaming."

"Sister, I'm looking up at the Boulevard. I love it up there. All of those people and the stars. I walk for hours looking at the names of all the people, all of the famous people. I hate it here. I have no friends, no one likes me."

"Give it time," she said as she touched my hair again.

"Yeah, right."

"I'm always over there," she said and pointed to the two-storied beige building.

"Thanks," I said.

"I'm Sister Ignatius."

"I'm Gracie."

"That name suits you, graceful and pure."

"You look more like an Iggy."

"Gracie, that was my nickname when I was your age. You can call me that, just don't let any of the other sisters hear you."

She stood up and went to the church. The lunch bell chimed off and recess began. I sat on my hands. They never invited me to play in the games. Even in PE, I was one of those who got thrown onto a side because they don't want to spend any more time deciding teams.

Today was a new day. I looked forward to today. It was hamburger day and I paid my thirty-five cents and bought one. And the books I ordered from Scholastic came in. And Iggy. When she stopped and talked to me, I wanted to tell her about the great books I was going to get. Sometimes she could be very religious, talking about God and stuff, but she was OK. I looked at her light brown eyelashes and small movements, practically like a china doll. She always held her hands together, like she was continually praying. Maybe she was praying for me.

Today the sun shone against the church and I soaked up the warmth of it. There was no sign of Iggy. I looked far off in the distance to the convent. The recess bell rang and the other boys and girls walked back into the school. I looked over at the convent and two men in dark suits and ties carried a long, black bag on a stretcher to the car.

"Gracie, that doesn't concern you," Sister Marie Jean said to me as she startled me with her rosy voice.

"What's going on, Sister?"

"Recess is over. It's time for you to get in. That doesn't concern you and you can't afford to miss any class time. You aren't that good a student."

When I looked at her, I swore the corners of her mouth curled up as she spoke to me. She appeared to be happy with the fact that I didn't care about my grades. I hated this school away from my real friends.

I didn't know what they were talking about when the other boys and girls talked to me. A couple of weeks ago, I came to school with my Kung Fu shoes on. Momma never came home that night. I left my saddle shoes in the Volvo after art class. I liked to sit in the backseat and put my feet out the window. I liked the way the air felt when Momma drove very fast. So, I wore my black Kung Fu shoes I got on the Boulevard. They were the only other shoes that I could fit. I was sitting on my favorite bench looking up at the Boulevard and then down at my shoes. I ate my glazed doughnut while wiping away the glazed sugar from the corners of my mouth, like I saw the ladies do at Musso and Frank. Maureen McGaffey walked over to me with her short black dirty hair and pig nose. She stuck out her just sprouting breasts and showed off her training bra through her white blouse.

"What are those?" she said pointing at my shoes.

"Shoes," I said.

"No, stupid. Where you from Gracie? The shoes, Gracie," she said. "Where you from?"

"I was born at Hollywood Presbyterian." I didn't understand the gang talk, I just liked the shoes.

"What a nerd," she said and walked away.

I got off of the bench and walked back to the school building. One of the Fathers I didn't know slammed shut the door to the station wagon he was loading boxes into. He seemed both preoccupied and upset. His nose was redder than it usually was.

I watched "Happy Days" last night and realized that Maureen McGaffey was very mean. I didn't know what she meant. I walked to class and my assigned seat. Because my last name was in the early part of the alphabet, I had to sit in the first row, third seat. I asked Mark what Maureen

McGaffey meant. Mark talked to me and he didn't mind that I was new this year. He sat behind me in class. His father worked on the Alaska Pipeline. He told me what it was like in Alaska. Cold and sunless. He told me that my Kung Fu shoes were gang shoes and that Maureen McGaffey was asking me what gang I was in. How stupid. Why didn't she just ask me? She's the nerd.

The P.A. system turned on and I heard Sister Inviolata clear her voice. She was the only one who spoke out of this creaky, wooden tulip-yellow painted box in our classroom.

"Children, attention children. Sister Ignatius died this morning. All classes are canceled this afternoon. We will attend a mass to pray for her. Please file out of your classrooms in an orderly manner. And let's remember we're in the house of God. Thank you."

I sat on the hard wooden chair and I wanted to cry, but I didn't show my weakness. Babies cry, that's what Nana said to me the only time I cried in front of her.

"Children, get your books together. We will have the quiz tomorrow, first thing in the morning."

I slammed my books together and threw them in my bookbag. One of the only people in this school who was nice to me was dead. I was mad.

This death thing, I didn't get it. Annie got to go to a funeral when one of Momma's relatives died. I got mad. They said I was too young to understand death. How stupid. You're not around anymore to eat, sleep and go to the bathroom.

Sister Marie Jean made us line up single file and walk to the church. She walked us to the side door of Blessed Sacrament Church. We walked in large double doors, past a rack of religious pamphlets with a black plastic sign saying donations 25 cents and a small closed can chained to the wall. I walked behind Susie Agnello and her very special blonde French braids. I delighted in one bad thought of burning them in the sacred candles. I dipped my fingers in the chipped pink and white marble bowl of holy water. The sediment at the bottom moved when my fingers touched the water. I made the sign of the cross and walked through a second pair of double doors, dirty brown vinyl with tarnished brass studs. We were all silent as we were led to the pews behind the fourth graders. I sat next to Susie and Carlos Campos. He liked Susie and she liked him. I sat in the middle.

"OW!" Susie screamed.

Sister Marie Jean was sitting in front of me. She turned around and gave me a dirty look. I looked at Carlos and he was laughing silently. Susie was laughing too. They thought it was funny.

"Hey, stop it," Susie screamed.

All of the other students in the church turned to stare at me. Sister Marie Jean wagged her finger at me.

During the mass, I stood. I sat. I got on my knees and held my hands together in empty prayer. I smelled the white burning wax in the chapels. I looked at the stations of the cross in their antique paint, and looked at the gold Roman numerals underneath them. Father Van Der Ahe was loud and forceful in his sermon for Iggy, as if the louder he got, the quicker she was going to heaven. He finished his words. We all said amen. Goodbye Iggy.

We stood up class by class and exited the church. We went back to the classroom and I took my seat behind Susie. Sister Marie Jean excused the class a minute early.

"Gracie, would you stay after?" she asked as she placed her right hand on my right shoulder.

All of the other kids walked out. Susie and Carlos laughed as they walked by me and slammed the door shut.

"Gracie, I know you're new to our school, but we have rules."

"I know."

"One of those is proper behavior in church. Church is the house of God. We do not misbehave in His house. Do I make myself clear?"

"But Sister Marie Jean."

"No buts, it is unladylike. Do I make myself clear?"

"Yes, Sister."

"That's better. Why don't you erase all the blackboards and then you can go home. Don't forget to study for the quiz tomorrow."

Sister Marie Jean pointed at the blackboards, picked up the books off of her desk and left the room. I walked to the blackboards and quickly erased them. My hands were covered in chalk dust and it was all over my uniform. I finished and picked up my bag. I walked out the door of the classroom and then out the doors that kept me in this school.

"Hey, Gracie."

I looked up and I saw Susie Agnello in her immaculately pressed uniform, still crisp after an entire day at school. When I looked at her in the sunlight, I saw that she was actually a very pretty girl. It looked like the sun's rays beamed out of the golden hair on her head.

"Yeah."

"Do you want to go to my house?"

"Where's Carlos?"

"That baby went home. Come on, let's go to my house. My parents won't be there. I have a pool; it'll be fun."

"Yeah, sure," I said. I knew that I was supposed to wait for Annie, but I didn't care. I wanted to get away from this school. I hated it here.

"Come on, my brother is waiting."

I followed Susie to a blue Volkswagen bug with a Rolls Royce grill welded to the front of it. The car was very confusing. There were two older boys, high school boys.

"Michael, this is Gracie. She's going to come over to the house."

"I don't care, get in."

I followed Susie into the backseat. We sat in the loudness of the radio and engine. I felt all grown up as I was being driven up the Boulevard by boys. We drove up Orange Drive and across Franklin. We passed my street and kept driving. We made a right turn on Outpost Drive. This section has bigger houses and large walls in front of the houses. The car stopped in front of a large gate; we sat in the car as the gate opened up. The car pulled in. Michael stopped the car and let me out of the backseat. Susie got out on her side, and I walked over and stood behind her.

"Hey stupid, what time will they be back?"

"Squirt, they're going to be late tonight. It's payroll."

"Great," Susie said.

I followed Susie to a large two-storied Spanish-style house. It was eggshell colored with a large garden filled with tiny pink flowers. She walked into the house and threw her bag and coat on the couch. I followed, but nicely placed my stuff next to hers. I followed her into the kitchen. I sat at the counter and watched Susie as she banged around the kitchen like a hurricane.

"Do you like that Sister Marie Jean?"

"No," I said. I finally got invited to a friend's house and all I could come up with was no. I should really tell her how I feel about that awful nun.

"I hate that school. I've been going there since the first grade. Those people are so weird. I see you at lunch sitting by yourself. I always wondered what you're doing over there. Now, where did they move that stuff."

Susie had the blender out on the counter in front of me. There were fresh red strawberries and ice cubes. She walks around the kitchen opening up cabinets.

"Now where did they move it? It's got to be around here somewhere." She stands up on a chair and opens the cabinet above the refrigerator.

"What are you looking for, Susie?"

"Here it is." She brought out a bottle of tequila. Susie got off the chair and walked to the counter. She placed ten ice cubes, two handfuls of strawberries, and one long pour of tequila into the blender.

"You watch this. I'll be right back."

Susie disappeared into the other room and I sat there watching the blender. The kitchen was sparkling clean. It didn't even look used. I walked over to a cabinet and opened it up. The plates were lined in rows atop yellow flowered paper. Every pile was straight. All of the rows of dishes were pyramid stacked.

"What are you doing?" Susie asked me.

"Oh, nothing," I said and sat back in my seat.

"You want one of these?" she said holding a pack of cigarettes.

"Sure," I said. I had never tried smoking. Momma did it. Daddy did it. It was such a grown-up thing to do.

"They're done," she said. She turned off the blender. Susie reached under the counter and brought out two large margarita glasses. She poured the pink slushie into the glasses and pushed one toward me.

"Thanks. What is it?" I asked.

"Just a margarita. Why don't we go out by the pool?"

"Susie, what about your brother and his friend."

"Let them make their own. They're too busy getting high and listening to the Stones in his room. That's all he ever does. He doesn't drink."

"And your parents?"

"Anthony and my step monster won't be back until late tonight. They have end of the month payroll."

"What about the alcohol?"

"OK, I almost forgot." Susie picked up the bottle of tequila and walked over to the sink. She put the bottle under the faucet and filled the bottle to the top with water.

"They'll think the maid did it. Let's go out by the pool and watch the sunset."

I followed Susie out of the kitchen through a side door. We walked outside to a winding green garden. The crunch of small grey pebbles echoed the silence high above the Boulevard. This path led to a large, rectangular pool. I followed Susie to a table with four directors chairs. They were bleached blue canvas with names across them. Susie sat in a chair marked Anthony. I sat next to her in a chair with the name Luisa.

"This is the life," Susie said.

"You're so lucky, to have this pool I mean."

"Want to go swimming, Gracie?" Susie said as she took out her pack of cigarettes and handed me one.

"I don't have a suit."

"Here, have a smoke. Let me figure this out."

I took the cigarette from her. She has already lit her cigarette. I fumbled with the matches, my hands shaking at such a grown-up thing to do. I ripped the match out of its book and ran the match against the striker. I dropped the match when it lit. Susie laughed at me. I tried it again and lit the cigarette this time. I inhaled the cigarette, just as I had seen my parents. And I choked. I felt all of the air get taken out of my lungs. I couldn't breathe. I inhaled the smoke, because I didn't want to look like a baby. I watched Susie inhale her cigarette and drink her slush. I imitated her, trying to look cool.

"This is the life," I said trying to sound cool.

We sat at the table and watched the sun slowly moving across the grey light of the hills. I took another sip of my slush and I felt warm. I stood up and walked over to the edge of the garden. A thick glass wall separated me from the other side. I felt like I was on the edge of the world. I looked down. The Boulevard looked small from here. That was the only thought I could come up with as my head started to spin and my cheeks were flushed and hot. It was the same flush of heat, my blushing, that came out when I was embarrassed. It was something I couldn't control.

"We don't need suits," Susie shouted in glee.

"Susie, there are boys here!" I shouted in modesty.

"No, silly. We can swim in our training bras and underwear."

"I don't want to."

"Don't be a baby, Gracie. Tell you what. You get in the pool and I'll go make sure that lousy brother of mine is out of the picture." Susie walked toward the house.

I started to unbutton my blouse. I wore an undershirt. I was undeveloped, not one of the lucky ones. I took off the blouse, then the skirt, and my shoes and socks. I tied my undershirt up and knotted it in front, so it looked like a bra. And I jumped in the water. It was warm and wonderful. I jumped up and down, the water was fun.

"He doesn't even answer his door."

"It's great. Susie, come in here."

I began to feel better, like I could fit in. I looked up at Susie. She stood in the reflection of the sun with her shimmery white training bra and little rosette in the middle of her chest and matching underwear. I looked down at my off-white undershirt and underwear, mended and torn so many times with Nana's stained yellow thread.

"Watch out!" she screamed as she jumps in the pool. She splashed and created a wave.

"That was great, Susie."

Susie rang the water out of her hair and looked at me strangely. I looked down at my unknotted undershirt.

"What's that, Gracie?"

"I don't wear a training bra yet."

"I thought everyone did in the fifth grade," she said floating on her back around the pool.

"Well, I don't."

"That's funny, Gracie."

"Susie, I have to go," I said as I rushed out of the pool. I was cold, dripped water on the chair, and felt humiliated.

"But no one can give you a ride," Susie stated so matter-of-factly.

"Susie, I'll walk. It's not that far." I held my clothes in my arms. I walked quickly from the patio to the gate. Susie screamed out something. I just keep walking. I walked out the gate, my feet covered in dirt and grey pebbles. I was in the street. I stood in the shadow of a bamboo tree and put on my unbuttoned blouse and threw my jumper on over it. I bent over to put on my shoes and a man with silver hair was staring at me from across the street. My head was pounding from the slush and I didn't want to ring the bell at the gate for Susie and my books. I was not a baby!

I started walking. I walked down the street. The man was behind me. I moved to the middle of the street and he was still there. He wore a long coat and a full-brimmed hat. I kept walking and I got down to Franklin. I stood at the light, waiting for it to turn green. I pushed the button. And I keep pushing the button, because I saw the man getting closer. There were so many cars, but I felt so alone. The light turned green. I ran across the street, between cars that had not stopped for the light. The man didn't catch the light. Half a block down, I turned around and a different old man was sitting on the bus bench. I ran down Franklin with the cars whizzing in my face, their colors were blurs. I got to Orchid and then crossed to my street. I ran up the street, happy to be home.

I walked into the house and into the bedroom. Annie was reading a book.

"Where were you, Gracie?"

"I went to Susie's house."

"Did you ask Momma. She's mad at you. And what happened to you? Look at you. You're dirty and you smell funny. You better take a bath before she finds you. She's on the warpath."

"I just want to get into bed." I crawled into the warmth of my covers and pee pee blanket.

Momma walked in our room and didn't knock. She walked loudly with her one-inch heeled, brown-speckled vinyl just-under-your-knee boots she got at Wild Pair last week.

"Annie, get on the piano."

"Let me finish this chapter, I'm almost done, Momma."

"No, Annie. Now."

"Just one more minute, Momma."

"What did I say, Annie?"

I listened to this and I didn't want to hear it. My head spun. The slush, the cigarette, and the man all zoomed around in my head.

"Leave her alone," I said from under my covers.

"What did you say, Gracie?" she pulled the covers off of me.

"Leave her alone," I said as I looked her in the eye.

"What happened to you? You're filthy. You smell like smoke. What are you on? What the hell have you been doing, and where have you been?"

"None of your goddamned business," I said as I borrowed a line from my father.

"You've been drinking; you're just like your father."

"I'm his daughter."

"We'll see about that, Gracie." Mom started to pace the room like a mad dog.

"Mom, leave her alone," Annie shouted.

"Stay out of this, and get to that piano, now!"

"She doesn't have to practice that stupid thing if she doesn't want to," Gracie snapped into the conversation.

"I've had enough of this," Mom said. She sat on my bed and took her boot off.

"No, Mom, not Gracie," Annie screamed, trying to distract her.

She took the boot in her right hand and with the heel hit me in the left eye. She broke skin under the eye. This slappy hit made no blood. I couldn't feel any blood falling. My mother broke out of her trance and started to cry. She reached over to hug me, rocking me back and forth. I felt like a rag doll in her arms, tearless and emotionless. She straightened out my hair and put her hand against my cheek, but I didn't feel it. Instead I felt the stinging pain under my eye.

"Look what you made me do, Gracie. I've ruined you. My angel, I have ruined you and all your beauty."

I looked over at Annie and she was crying. Crying because she never thought I would be touched the same way she had been touched. I was a rag doll being rocked back and forth, not feeling anything. My mother dropped me on the bed and ran out of the room. I looked over at Annie and her tear-filled eyes. I would not cry. I went to sleep thinking about tomorrow and my day with my father.

I woke up early with the cold in our room. We never closed the window because it was broken; it didn't close all of the way. I reached under the bed for my pink-and-blue-flowered jewelry box. The small, pink ballerina started to dance to the music when I opened it up. I ripped the dancer off her stage, but the box still played. I looked into the diagonal square mirror at my eye. It was a blueish brown, with one tiny drop of blood under the skin, an internal bruise of the cheek.

I got up and went to the bathroom to draw a bath. I peeled off my dirty uniform and undershirt and underwear and left them on the floor. I got into the bath and sat there. I had some strange notion that I could scrub all that was wrong with me off. Shampoo. Rinse. Repeat. When it was time get out and look in the mirror, there was no change. I used the No More Tears Detangler on my hair, but I still wanted to cry about yesterday. I still had so many tears. I used my lavender water in a pretty little white porcelain bottle with a purple bow around its neck. I put on my peasant dress, white with an orange check skirt. I placed two barrettes in my hair, on both sides of my face. Perhaps they would distract from the main event in the middle of my face. And I wore my favorite Kung Fu shoes with white lacy socks. It was eight-thirty in the morning and I sat on the front porch staring at the street, waiting for Daddy.

He would take us wherever we wanted to go. And we could order whatever we wanted. He never sat down to eat with us, but he always came back to check on us. He called us his "two little darlings."

I stared at the spider web under our bedroom window. And at the dust on the shiny white paint. It was Saturday morning and I didn't feel like watching cartoons with Annie. I sat on the porch. I heard the screen door slam; it was Momma. She walked over and sat next to me on the stairs.

"Gracie, angel, how are you?"

"I'm fine," I said staring at the seams in the concrete.

"Baby, we have to get something straight. I didn't mean to hit you; you made me do it. You made me so mad, just like your father. I don't want you to tell your father or grandfather how this happened. They won't understand. I promise it won't happen again. I'll make it up to you. I promise I'll make it up to you."

"You want me to lie, Momma? It's a sin, you know," I lectured.

"Not lie, just make up a story. Say you slipped running up the stairs. Please, sugar. I'll make it up to you."

"Fine, if you say so," I agreed.

"Thanks, baby," she said as she kissed my forehead.

She stood up and I heard the terry cloth from her flowered robe brush the concrete. She walked inside, the screen door slapping the frame. She stuck her head out the door.

"Baby, you want some Cream of Wheat? I'll make it fluffy, just the way you like it. And I'll put brown sugar and butter, your favorites," Momma said. She was trying to get me to her side. But I'm Daddy's girl. I always will be. Forever.

"No, thanks. Daddy's taking us to lunch at Musso and Frank."

I sat on my stair and waited for Daddy. The sun changed directions as I sat there all day. I sat in my Kung Fu shoes waiting for Daddy. The sun went down, and the night blooming jasmine began to spray its magical perfume. I walked back inside to my room. I hung my dress over the chair and took off my socks, delicately placing them inside each shoe. I must have gotten the days mixed up. He'll be here soon. Or maybe tomorrow. Maybe I got the days mixed up again.

Snapshot
Musso & Frank

When I was very young, I only ate roast beef sandwiches. M & F made the best sammies on white bread with mayo. One day Annie mooed the entire time we were having lunch to remind me that roast beef comes from cows. It was a low moo that was hard to pick up on so close to the bar, but I did. Finally, Mommy yelled at her, but it was too late. So now ham sandwiches were all I will ever eat there. Plain ham, no mayo, no lettuce, no tomato on white bread dry. And a ginger ale. Sometimes a Shirley Temple. Other days a Roy Rogers was what I drank. The waiters never acted like I was ordering anything strange.

Only men wait tables I noticed. They kept us in a booth facing the bar. Red and Mia liked to keep an eye on us while they sat up at the bar.

The long ride home was the worst. Red crossed the lines and almost hit the cars parked along the street. Momma was usually dozing off with her head resting against the window glass. She didn't see the California roll he did at Yucca.

A red light pulled behind us and I heard a short siren and saw a flashing light.

Red was busted for drunk driving. I watched him miss his nose when he was doing another field sobriety test. Mommy begged the officers to let her take Daddy home.

Daddy was placed in the backseat of the police car. Momma drove us up Las Palmas back up to the hills. Daddy didn't come home that night.

Snapshot
Santa Monica Beach

I was the queen of the monkey bars. Chalked up the palms to absorb the sweat. Jumped the bottom step. Climbed on with both hands. Glided through the air in a circular leap. Ring to ring to ring. I flew through the air with the salt water misting my face. Annie was not paying attention to me; but she was talking to some guy.

Annie always got the attention of guys. I never knew how she did it. Perhaps it was her chestnut hair and those deep, brown eyes. I didn't have the gift to make people get lost in my eyes. Sabra and Hannah had that same quality as well. Everyone saw it when they walked down the Boulevard together, heads turned and necks craned. The girls lived in the apartments down on Franklin. The pool on Franklin was behind a cinder block fence. They sat in the pool and listened to all of life driving by them. Sabra and Hannah had been friends for a while. They wore white crocheted bikinis and laid out on the chaise lounges in the sun. They were both only thirteen.

Snapshot
Penny Lane

There was always a line of big, chrome motorcycles in front of this dark head shop. I didn't make eye contact but I had to walk past the not very well-lit pipe shop to get to Two Guys from Italy on the Boulevard. The one on Yucca doesn't sell slices like this one does. Gotta get my slice. Some afternoons I would see Sabra and Hannah walking down the Boulevard delivering their small bags of weed. Life from the front window was like a television show, so much action taking place.

No eye contact. I looked at all of the black leather they wore year-round. There was a story there.

Momma said everyone had a story. These people have a story. She wrote the stories for songs in other people's music. But she never got credit. This was because someone was paying her for help. Momma said Penny Lane was a song by the Beatles. She said the song had a story in it like all songs. But Momma said the Beatles were not very good musicians, and they were rude to the Queen.

Snow White and the Queen Mary Plate

He had a new home, an apartment on Los Feliz Boulevard. Wasn't that great? All the way through Hollywood and across Franklin, we traveled in his car. Me, I was sitting in the middle and trying to hang my head as far away from his Tiparillo. The Grand Prix he drove had a hole in the middle of the floor in the front seat from where the stick shift used to be. A mechanic changed the car from stick shift to automatic. So then I watched the grey black grooves in the street. I held his Mickey Big Mouth, both hands squeezing the emerald green barrel.

Gracie and I don't talk to one another today. I'm mad at her. Sometimes I get mad at her because she is the baby. And other times I just get mad at her. I don't know. I get tired of the stupid questions and her baby talk. I get tired of her long blonde hair and how perfectly like a doll she looks. Sometimes as we play in the backyard among the laurel trees, I think I can almost hear them singing my name. It is like I am special again and I don't have anyone to share the spotlight.

Yesterday I was sitting on the wooden bench in the backyard. Gracie and I were playing jacks. I got my onesies, twosies, and threesies. Then I missed. She laughed. I took her by her corn yellow hair and banged her head against the wooden bench. I kept doing it three or four times, until I saw the blood coming from her nose. She ran inside the house. I continued to play jacks. That got boring by myself, so I went inside to see what Gracie was doing. I went into the bedroom. Gracie stood on a chair with her arms stretched out the window. In her hand was my Snow White.

"No, don't!"

"Yes!"

"Please don't do it, Gracie."

"Yes, I'm gonna do it, Annie."

"No, Gracie, I'm sorry."

I should have remembered what it was like to get on her bad side. The golf club incident came into my mind. Last month, I called her a stupid whiny baby. I was outside trying to tan my pale skin. She came outside with her green plastic golf club and missed my head by two inches. I didn't think it was an accident; I just thought she was a bad shot. Lack of coordination and all that stuff I hear Mom and Nana talk about.

"I'm gonna do it," she said swinging Snow White around like she was Superman.

"Please, no."

It was the one thing in life Daddy bought for me and I liked it. I loved Snow White. She sat on the table by my bed, and at times I believed I was Snow White. It was one present I really liked, not like the others from Daddy. He gave us Mickey Mouse watches with bright shiny red bands. I lost mine in the ivy at school. He gave us autographed pictures of the guys from "Bonanza," but I didn't know who they were. I crayoned on mine, because I felt they all looked better with green mustaches, red horns, and black teeth. Daddy was like that; he would bring us presents for no reason.

But on holidays it was different. He always gave us money orders, never cash. What does he expect us to do with those things anyway? We made paper airplanes and sailed them to the roof.

I looked at her angry eyes, hoping she would stop playing with my Snow White.

"Gracie, don't do it, please."

"OK," she said as she looked me in the eye with her angry green eyes. She dropped Snow White. Snow White fell to the ground. I heard Snow White crumble as she hit the concrete on that fifteen-foot drop. I never went out to pick up the pieces. I wanted them to blow away.

Daddy drives up to the big apartment with a Hawaiian name on Los Feliz. It's black and white with big glass doors. This is his home, now.

"We're here," he said.

"Goody," Gracie yells and jumps up and down on the seat.

"Oh great," I said.

We get out of the car and follow behind him. Gracie hands me her bag from the Queen Mary we got with Mom yesterday. In the bag is a red, white and blue picture plate of the Queen Mary. She hands me the bag and runs up to catch Daddy's hand. I look at her smiling at him as I trail behind them. We walk around a sky-blue pool. I want to hold his hand too. I want to be a special little girl, just like Gracie. I run to catch up with them. My foot catches on a yellow and white striped pool chair. As I fall, the plate crashes in the bag and breaks into a million pieces. I cannot stop my fall hard on the concrete. I stay down, paralyzed from the hard fall. I look at Gracie, crying as she walks next to me and picks up the tattered bag. Our father walks over to her and puts his arm around her. He wipes her tears with his large magnificent hand. I am lying on the concrete with two scraped knees filled with gravel and blood. My father reaches his hand out to me. I quickly get up and he puts his arm around me. I am under his wing.

Snapshot
JJ Newberry's

S itting at the bus stop to wait for her, always waiting for Mom. Annie disappeared into the store to buy some big Bazooka bricks, bubblegum flavored. Mom went in to get her hair dye, whatever red was on sale is the red she used. I wished she was more like Prudy's mom who lets her grey hair grow only to her ears. Gamine was what I heard my mom compliment her on. A little boy haircut was what I thought it looked like, but easy peasy.

As I kicked my feet under the concrete bench and looked at the picture of Frankenstein complete with bolts in either side of his neck advertising the Hollywood Wax Museum on the board behind me. I saw them walking. They were holding hands, then they were walking arms locked together. They wore the same outfit — dark blue jeans, Nike courts (white perforated leather, barely worn), and long-sleeved purple-striped shirts.

"What are you looking at little girl?" asked one of the men who snickered at me.

The two men looked at each other and laughed, returning to hand holding as they loudly laughed and hollered down the Boulevard.

I slid down the bus bench until I was eye level with Frankenstein and Marilyn Monroe on the bench still waiting.

Supply Sergeant

Everything in this store was either army green, black or camouflage. I liked looking at the Swiss Army knives under the glass display case at the front counter. Mom dragged me in to buy a canteen for summer camp. I kept saying "She's too young to go. She's six," but Mom insisted that she needed to have some time to herself and think things out.

While Mom and Gracie paid for everything, I stepped outside to the Boulevard. I wished I had enough time to run over to the candy shop. I loved the hand-rolled fudge. The large marble slabs where the old guy rolled the fudge, which was cold to the touch.

One day as Gracie and I leaned into the slabs, the candy guy invited us behind the counter. With teeth missing from his smile he had the appearance of a harmless jack-o-lantern. Gracie stared in a trance at the rock candy lollipops. When the old man walked by me, he motioned his finger for me to follow him into a back area behind a curtain where I had never been before. Just as I went through the curtain he grabbed my hand, but I pulled back just in time to catch the sight of an old army cot behind the curtain. Suddenly, the store bell rang and Gracie was released from her candy trance and started to scream out my name. Sometimes when I'm walking the Boulevard, I look over at the candy shop and I see him smiling at me with his missing teeth.

The Pussycat Theater was next door to the Supply Sergeant. "Deep Throat" was the movie on the marquis. It never changed. I stood next to the glass poster cases. There was a bright yellow poster with a picture of a woman in three poses with her halter top and bikini bottoms. Her arms were raised up in the last pose which was closest to the front. I thought it was a movie about dancing. But it didn't look like my ballet poses with Madame Etienne.

Coming out of the Supple Sergeant, my mother put her wallet inside her purse and gathered up Gracie to get us back home. But that was not before Gracie was pulling my mom to a gumball machine and my mom was hunting around the bottom of her purse for some coins. Sometimes watching Gracie was like watching a television show, minus the laugh tracks.

A guy in a trench coat walked up to me as I leaned against the movie case. I tried to look cool, like Sabra and Hannah, my Hollywood girl crushes. He opened his coat while walking by me. I saw his penis on his way inside the theater. My mother walked up to me oblivious and the guy walked quickly to the ticket window. Gracie was stuck at the gumball machine, trying to twist more candy and gum out of it than she had paid for. I was the only one to see Mr. Trenchcoat.

Snapshot
The Ontre Cafe

"Billy Barty is shorter than me," I whispered to Annie. "If I sneezed, I could surely land it on top of his head."

"Shush," she said as she elbowed me. He was standing right in front of me.

I started to line up all of the juices like they would run across all of the stainless-steel racks. Saran Wrap trapped all of the tomato-prune-grapefruit-orange. Super old people drank the prune. Billy Barty drank the orange juice.

I hated coming here and having to walk by the old people who made eating look like a sport. I thought of Nana and I knew she must have had just as difficult a time chewing her food. So that was why we shared a Bavarian cream pie. Softness. Chocolate cream. Maraschino cherries. But I never ate the cherries, not since Daddy Red took me to the cocktail lounge before the flight to Vegas. I thought it was a place to rest. Twenty-five maraschino cherries later, my stomach was a mess.

He thought I wasn't very good at counting his five drinks, when he said he only had two. But I knew how to count and he didn't. All over Mom's tan velour Levi bell bottoms, I let the cherries go. She wasn't happy on the trip. I knew it was my fault, but I just couldn't keep them down. She never wore those pants again after I vomited all over them.

Snapshot
Peaches

Music blared out of the life-sized speakers placed outside of this record store on the Boulevard. Elton John and his Crocodile Rock. Kiss and Saturday Night. Bruce Springsteen and Thunder Road. All musical lyrics tell a story, according to my mom.

I loved to flip through the peach crates full of records. Flipping through the vinyl covers each one a work of art, each cover told a pre-story to the stories inside about to be released.

When I saw Sabra and Hannah twirling their hair and dancing in front of the clerks, I had to walk into the store. They always seemed so free, their hips in sync with one another, white crocheted bikini tops and blue jean cut-offs with flip flops. I wanted to be that perfect and that loved and that popular when I am older.

Hannah handed the boy behind the counter a tiny baggie from her palm as they turned a perfect circle, two girls in one another's arms, California dreaming

Daisy

I heard my grandmother curse in Hungarian at Momma slamming the door on her way out on this Saturday night. I sat in the kitchen with her soaking up the heat from the stove because the wall heater in the front room doesn't work. We didn't use the old stone fireplace. There was an underlying dampness in the house, probably because we're not quite in the hills, but the foothills. My Momma left every Saturday night to play piano at The People Tree on Sunset Boulevard. I couldn't go there because they don't serve food like the places Daddy takes us to eat.

Nana banged the pots and pans in her own private world. I pretended not to notice, but I was glad there was someone here with me.

"Anna, do you want something to drink?" Nana asked as if suddenly remembering me.

"Yes," I said, having to remember that she was talking to me. Nana refused to call me Annie, because she wanted my mother to name me after her favorite sister, Anna. My mother refused, something about it being too old world. Nana went so far as to try to change it at the hospital, but they wouldn't listen to her in the records department. They probably thought she was crazy with her navy blue Keds, rolled down knee highs, and polyester thrift store dress.

"Yes, what?" she asked me, giving the look.

"Yes, please, Nana."

"You girls are not being taught right. You need your mother here. No manners," she said shaking her head.

I looked at her and she looked so serious. Her long white hair was pulled so tight in a bun, never more than ten strands dared sneak out of that bun. She pulled her hair up every morning and only let it down in the darkness of her bedroom. One night I listened at the door as the hair pins clinked against her room. Her wire framed glasses made deep indents in the sides of her nose, and she wore them too, until the lights went out, and then she tucked them under her pillow for safe keeping.

"Yes, pretty please, Nana."

"Anna, do you want milk or Tang?"

"Can I have soda pop, Nana?"

"No, you can't."

"Please, Nana."

"No, Anna don't whine. It's not pretty. Your father spoiled you with that soda pop. He gives you girls everything you want. What a man, ha."

"Can I have Tang, please?"

"Yes."

Nana reached into the cabinet above the sink. She picked up the jar of Tang, put a teaspoon full in my Josie and the Pussycats glass, ran tap water, and put it on the table. The phone rang and she went to answer it in the other room. I didn't run for the phone because I didn't have any friends to call me. I tasted the Tang and it tasted like orange flavored water. She was always light on the Tang. I put another spoonful in my glass, a heaping spoonful. Then I walked over to the piggy cookie jar, put three cookies in my hand and stuffed three others in my mouth, because the rule for me was only three cookies at a time. Mom believed in rules for everything. She said that it would help us in the real world when we grew up, if we obeyed all of the rules.

"Only three cookies, Anna, I heard you open the jar. Be a good girl," Nana called out from the living room.

"Yes, Nana," I said.

I didn't use a napkin and I flipped three cookies onto the table. They broke apart and made crumbs. They looked like big and small rocks, metamorphic

I believe, born out of an explosion. I opened my notebook and looked at what I had for homework. I wished I had gone to the slumber party with Gracie. Trudy's mom said I could come, but I pretended like I had something to do, because I didn't want a pity invitation. That's what I always get as the fat girl. All of Gracie's' friends' mothers feel sorry for me, and invite me. I said yes one time and stayed up late to watch Saturday Night Live with Trudy's older brother while they did hair and make-up all night long. I'm not one of those girly-girls; I'm a tomboy.

My assignment book said capitals of the states. I looked at my consolation, my three cookies and saw a cockroach on the rocks of crumbs.

"Are you doing your homework, Anna?" Nana called out.

"Yes."

"What did you say?" She said prodding me for the response she wanted to hear.

"Yes Nana. I'm doing my homework."

I looked at my new friend. I decided she was a girl like me. I would call her Daisy.

"Hello Daisy."

"What did you say Anna?" Nana screamed from the other room.

"Nothing, Nana."

"Hello Daisy, I'm pleased to meet you," I whispered.

I broke off some more crumbs, she was brave. Daisy didn't run from the wave of my hand.

"Daisy, this is the fate of the fat girl. Nothing to do on a Saturday night and no one to do it with. I didn't mean you, I'm sorry. At least if Gracie was here, I could bug her. Ha...that's a joke. Bug her and you're a cockroach. The capital of California is Sacramento. Daisy, I bet you didn't know that."

I looked at Daisy's dark brown tentacles. Quick. She was very fast. She had no friends like me, because she was all alone. Her mother spent days going out and looking for food, and her father left home because he was bad. She didn't have any brothers or sisters, so she was quite lucky.

"Anna, are you doing your homework?" Nana yelled from the other room.

She always knew when I was off task.

"Yes, Nana."

I broke off more crumbs for my new friend.

"Daisy my new friend. I'm going to take you everywhere, you can go with me to school, and I can show everyone. It'll be great, we can go down to the Boulevard and hang out. I'll get you some candy and popcorn. Those are my favorites. I'm not sure what you drink, but I'll buy you as much soda pop as you can drink.

"What are you doing, Anna?" Nana said walking back into the room.

"Nothing, Nana."

"I heard you talking in here. I have to keep my eye on you all of the time, Anna. I couldn't even enjoy the conversation on the phone because you were talking."

"Sorry, Nana. I'm just memorizing the capitals out loud. It helped me."

"Look at that," Nana said. She took her hand and crushed Daisy with her right hand.

My new friend was dead.

"You killed Daisy," I said to her accusingly.

"What?" she asked.

"Never mind, Nana."

"Your mother is no housekeeper. She is a dirty woman. The next thing you know, we'll have rats and mice." She said as she wiped off the table and the remains of my new friend.

"Really?" I said as I put the last cookie in my pajama pocket and went to my bedroom.

Snapshot
The Hillside Strangler

There were bodies of young, nude girls popping up all over Hollywood and Los Angeles. Everyone was on edge. I only know this because I snuck out to the front room one night while Red was sleeping in his lounger chair. The news was on and it talked about The Hillside Strangler. Then on TV it showed pictures of dead bodies of girls posed and naked on the local hillsides.

The priest blessed our necks at the First Friday Mass. He held two candles together in an X shape at the base of our necks and we kneeled. After he blessed us, we responded with "Thank You, Father." The Blessed Sacrament saved us.

This morning Mom said she was giving us a ride to school today. Gracie ran into the front seat, so I climbed into the back seat and slammed the door shut. Mom gave me a side glance. I ignored her glance. Off we rode in the old Volvo she loved dearly.

Waiting for the light to change, I watched Sabra and Hannah in their white crocheted bikinis with two older guys. The cinder blocks of the privacy fence around the small pool made it difficult to see their faces completely, but I recognized their identical white crocheted bikinis.

Both of the guys had dark hair and moustaches. Their blue work shirts reminded me of the workers inside of Pep Boys down at Gower. How funny they don't wear trunks to go into the pool.

The older guy moved the hair off of Hannah's face. Sabra was lying next to the younger guy. I couldn't see anyone else around the pool.

The light changed and out onto Franklin we traveled. I wondered why the girls weren't going to school. Maybe they graduated from Le Conte Junior High. Perhaps they were already at Hollywood High School which was just down the street. But they would be late for Homeroom. I hoped they had a good day at school. Maybe I would be able to catch up with them later.

Copycat

I always brought everything home to Annie. She always appeared to stay clean. I was the younger and noisier. She was tight lipped. There were days when I asked her about the time she ran away, but she just ignored me. She pretended that she couldn't hear me by putting her hands over her eyes, her ears and her mouth, like she had a gigantic secret between herself and God. I got jealous and I got mad. She just kept moving her hands from her eyes, to her ears, and then to her mouth, over and over again.

Finally, I brought home chicken pox. It was the least I could do.

"Gracie, what are you doing?" Momma asked as I was wiping my first sore on Annie's arm exactly where I had one on my arm.

We always wanted to be twins and now was the chance.

"Nothing," I said, scared at her harsh tone.

Days later Annie had her own sore. And then they bloomed all over her body, like kisses from

God. I had a playmate for my illness; and it was much better than being all alone. Nana had this thought that being sick should not be fun. She made us sit in the darkness of the bedroom without television, listening to all the outside noises of the day, the laughter and playing of imaginary friends who had fun. But with the two of us, Nana just let the two of us run around the house in our t-shirts and underwear, itching ourselves on the arms of the sofa and loveseat, and the piano and piano bench. I lifted the piano bench top up and put my arm in the crease, with the weight I left it in the crease and itched all of the sores until they were bloody, and then I picked off the old scabs and waited for the new ones to dry. Annie said I was sick, but then she did the same thing after I was gone. Copycat.

Annie was older than me, but I had more friends. I think it was because she was big and scary. I loved my sister; I just didn't like her most of the time. But she was always around, so at least I had someone to play with.

Since I got sick first, Annie was still in the house itching her sores on the piano bench. I just watched, so smart because I could go out of the house now and she couldn't. I was smarter. I got it first.

I watched the morning glory's wind around our redwood fence and I wanted to be that pretty when I grew up. Or at least as pretty as Jane, the girl up the street. She lived above a garage in an apartment to the largest house up on the hill. I looked at Annie, all caught up in the misery of her chicken skin, and I walked up the street to see if Jane was home. She was sitting outside on her front porch. I could feel Annie staring at me through the screen door, no doubt her face pushed up against the mesh.

"Hey there, Gracie," said Jane.

"Hello Jane," I said as I sat next to her.

She was wearing short jean cutoffs and a pink t-shirt that said 99% Angel and 1% Devil. I had no idea that Jane was religious; she didn't wear a crucifix like the other girls at church do. She smelled like white flowers, like gardenias.

"What are you doing all the way up here Gracie?"

"What are you doing out here?" I asked, ignoring the question that would only make me have to go back home.

"Well I'm reading. You know you look better. I heard you got chicken pox. It didn't seem to ruin that beautiful face," she said as she touched my chin.

"What are you reading?"

"It's a book by F. Scott Fitzgerald, *The Great Gatsby*. It's a great book. I thought there might be a part in it for me. They're starting to cast the movie next week."

"How can there be a part in a book for you?"

"Gracie, I'm an actress. I know they're doing the movie. I hope to make it big one day. I want to have my own star on the Boulevard."

"I've done modeling. I'm pretty good on the runway. It's not very fun, I don't like it much. Momma was the one who liked it."

"Gracie, you never know. When you start out young, sometimes it can be better. Otherwise you have to work odd jobs and do things you wouldn't do, just to get money. But you wouldn't know about stuff like that, you're so young."

As she talked, she played with my braids. I just stared into her beautiful face.

"What are you doing tonight, Jane?"

"I've got a friend coming over to pick me up. There's a big party. He's a big Hollywood producer, and he may have a part for me in his next movie."

"You'll get it Jane. You're so pretty ... and talented."

"What are you going to do tonight, Gracie?"

148

"Dee Dee's away at her Dad's. Mom plays the bar tonight. No fun at all tonight. I mean Annie is there, but now she has the pox. Oops."

"Do you want to come inside while I get dressed?"

"Sure," I blurted out. I had never been inside her home. I knew it had to be a cool place.

Jane got up and walked into her apartment. She swayed her hips back and forth, like a big cat. Her hair moved. She had a movie star look to her. I was finally excited to be going into the place. From the front door window, I always saw an amber music box on her table. I wanted to be like her when I grew up. As I was about to follow her inside, I heard a familiar sound.

"GRACIE…GRACIE!!! Come home now! NOW!!!" Nana screamed up the street.

"I'd better go. Have a great night tonight, Jane. I hope you get the part!" I said as I walked out the door and ran down the block.

I never saw Jane again. A week went by before I saw any movement in her apartment. I heard Jane never came back from her date. There was a police car parked in her driveway. I walked my bicycle passed her driveway and up to the top of the hill. On garbage day, I bicycled up the hill and when I came down, in the garbage was Jane's amber music box and her copy of *The Great Gatsby*. Painters went in a couple of days later and the For Rent sign was taped to the window. Someone else lives there now.

Snapshot
Ye Rustic Inn

Having a Sunday afternoon Daddy, like Dee Dee, looked and sounded great. She went to the Merry-go-round and the train every weekend in Griffith Park. Then they spent the rest of the afternoon in Beverly Hills shopping, since her father got a job as a writer on "Hart to Hart." Dee Dee complained that her step monster Wendy always came with them, so she had to sit in the back seat of the Mercedes. She had to sit quietly as they dined at Perino's and talked to one another about plot, scene direction and dialogue.

When Wendy brought me along as a number two, we went to private homes. Dee Dee and I usually hung by the pool and the house servants got us Pepsi and made us sandwiches. Ham sandwiches. The adults were usually upstairs, laughing and smoking. Weird smells floated down to the pool. This was the life for Dee Dee.

My Sunday afternoons ended over at the Rustic. The bartender Rick kept comic books for me and Annie. But lately she refused to come and hang out with me and Archie and Jughead and Betty and Veronica. I was never alone, even without her.

Cinnamon Toast

"I hate you!" Gracie screamed at Nana and Annie as she was being pulled down the street and up on the porch, and lastly being shoved into the house by Nana.

"So what, I don't care!" Annie screamed back pulling Gracie's pigtails.

"You should be home where you belong, you little brat. You're too young to be at Dee Dee's house all the time. Get into your bedroom and don't come out until you're a nice girl," screamed Nana. Her face was in a rage and her eyes bulged from her anger.

"Forget it," I screamed as I ran into my bedroom, slammed the door, and hid in the bed with my shoes on. I hugged Dolly under the weight of my covers.

The door burst open and I felt the glare of Nana's eyes. I could see her sockless Keds standing in front of me. Her whole round body shook as she sat on the bed. I couldn't move.

"What did you say, Gracie?"

"I hate you!"

"No, after that. I won't put up with foul language from you. I'm not your mother and you can't play sweet little girl with me. You devil child. You're just like her when she was your age. Do your homework!"

"No, I won't!"

"Fine. You just sit here in the dark until you become a nice little girl again."

"Forget it. Get out! Ouch!" before I could move, Nana hit me. Under the covers my skin stung. She hit me with her open hand, and created a stinging hot welt.

"You made me do that. You just stay here, Gracie, for the rest of the night. Bad girls don't get rewards!"

Nana got up off of the bed, walked out the door, and slammed it. I could hear her angry Keds stomping away. I looked at my leg by the fading evening light. A shiny pink glow with the imprint of her fingers was on my leg. It was warm to the touch. I don't cry. I was not a crier. I would not give Nana the satisfaction of hearing me cry.

I got out of bed and looked at Dee Dee's house. Her house was white with a candy pink trim. Dee Dee's mother, Wendy, was ordering pizza for us tonight for dinner. Pepperoni and extra cheese. Two Guys from Italy was my favorite. But Nana dragged me home. She always dragged me home. Nana took me out of Wendy's because Nana didn't like her. Dee Dee was my best friend. Nana thought that Wendy should be married. I heard her tell Mom that Wendy doesn't wear a bra. And she had men visit her. They left envelopes. She slept until noon some days. She was a model; she was very pretty. Blonde. Thin. Tall. Young. Their house smelled like tea roses. When I went over to play with Dee Dee, I thought I was in a garden. Their house was fun. Wendy and Dee Dee always laughed. They smiled. They talked. I always had a fun time with them. I never wanted to go home.

Wendy made muslin dolls and lamps. For my last birthday, Dee Dee and Wendy gave me a doll. I called her Dolly. She was five feet tall and cushy. Dolly was faceless with pink hair.

I heard Nana banging pots and pans in the kitchen. My room was dark. I saw the lights from Dee Dee's house. Then I watched the pizza be delivered. Annie was watching the "Wonderful World of Disney," because I just heard the introduction. I sat in the darkness on the end of the bed because I couldn't get comfortable.

I opened the window and climbed out. I walked in white socks against the hard pebbles of the stone path that linked our two homes. As I looked into their front room, candles were lit on the mantle. Wendy poured an old man wine, blood-colored wine. She sat next to him on the couch. She was laughing and glowing against the dancing candles. I walked in the wet soil and looked into Dee Dee's room. She was sitting in front of the television watching "The Wonderful World of Disney." She ate a slice of pepperoni pizza and drank a Coke. I walked back across the pebbles to my house, climbed in the window, and got into bed with my dirty socks on. I fell asleep.

The singing crickets outside my window woke me up. After taking off my dirty socks and hiding them under the bed, I walked through the unlit house. Annie was asleep on the couch. She had her pink and green boo boo blanket wrapped around her body. Nana was in the kitchen. There were travel brochures on Hungary and Northern Europe on the table.

"Do you want some toast, Gracie?"

"Please, Nana," I said. I sat in the chair and looked at the green land and pictures of people I didn't even know.

"Do you want some milk?"

"Yes please, Nana."

She stood at the sink scrubbing the rust rings and scratches from the cast iron skillets she used. The white toast popped up. She buttered it and cut in half for me. Then Nana poured a glass of milk in my favorite Scooby-Dooby Doo glass. She knew it was my all-time favorite glass.

"Can you make it cinnamon toast please, Nana?"

She picked up the plate and placed it on the counter. She opened the cabinet and took out her magical mixture. Then she brought the toast back to me.

"Thanks," I said softly.

Nana sat in the chair opposite me, drinking Postum and dipping her cinnamon toast. I drank my milk and dipped my cinnamon toast too. It was after midnight and Mom was not home. The two of us sat in the kitchen eating toast in the silence of the Hollywood Hills.

Snapshot
Grauman's Chinese Theater

"If I get the plastic gold Grauman's salt and pepper shakers for Mom's birthday, everything will be ok."

"No, it won't, stupid," Annie said.

"Don't call me stupid. It's mean. I'm not dumb."

"Right. You're a blonde," Annie said, then proceeded to kick over the baby doll carriage filled with escargot shells Gracie had bought at a neighbor's garage sale. As Gracie ran after them like damaged babies, Annie watched her lovingly pick up each shell, wipe it on her t-shirt and place it back in the carriage.

Annie is older than me but she still thinks of me as a baby. That's probably because she doesn't like me getting older. Mom told me a story that when they brought me home from the hospital, Annie took care of me. I was her living and breathing doll. She changed, fed, and burped me like she was a nanny. It was so long ago that I don't remember any of it. I never remembered things.

"Five twenty-five, not including tax," the lady said suspiciously. For weeks, I have visited this gift shop eyeballing the salt and pepper shakers. I thought that Mom would love these so much. I haven't liked anything this much since the white macramé purse at that store The Orient near Cherokee. I handed her six dollars.

"Keep the change," I said like Red who always said that to our waitresses.

She handed me these real Hollywood souvenirs and Mom's happiness was in the palm of my hands. Mom was still sleeping when I got home. I wouldn't tell her that I nearly got myself killed on Franklin and Orchid crossing without a light, while some guy just started yelling at me in the middle of the street. And I almost dropped the shakers, but they were safely in the palm of my hand.

Let's Go Shopping

Hollywood was our territory. Auntie Nan lived on Gower Street just above Franklin Avenue, in a small studio apartment across the street from the Monastery of the Angels. There were cloistered nuns in the monastery, but I had never seen any nun from behind the tall, black iron gates. Some days I was over at Auntie Nan's and I could hear the single bell tolling throughout Beachwood Canyon. Auntie Nan never answered any of my questions about the monastery.

Auntie Nan was always busy. She sang and danced and performed. She played folk guitar in a candle-lit room in the basement of the church down the block from our house. "The Methodists" was how I overheard Momma refer to them. She knitted afghans and had ponchos in every color of the earth-toned rainbow. Auntie Nan had long red hair and when she drove with the top down in her car, it blew every which way but in her face. I watched her through my red heart-shaped sunglasses and smiled as she changed gears with her brown racing gloves on her oh so teeny, tiny hands. Auntie Nan just finished college; she graduated from UCLA. Mom and Auntie Bean did too, but I was there to see Auntie Nan in her black robes. She wanted to go to New York and be famous. I think she will. When I grow up, I want to be small and thin, just like Auntie Nan.

Auntie Nan loved to go shopping. She slowly walked around, going from shop to shop. She shopped for mini's and long-tiered skirts on the far-left side of the sizes, the smallest because she was so petite. Auntie Nan didn't say anything about my weight, like Auntie Bean. I'm big for my age, husky like Mom said, and fat like I heard Auntie Bean call me in the middle of the night when I sat outside her kitchen door and heard her talk to Uncle Steve about me. Auntie Nan doesn't get embarrassed when we shopped in the big girl's section. I love Auntie Nan.

Auntie Nan was over at our house talking to Mom in the kitchen. Auntie Nan looked so cute today; she came into my bedroom before she went into the kitchen to visit with Mom. I liked her because she talked to me and she smelled of that Maja perfume she always wore. The Spanish Flamenco dancer was on the box in a red and black dress. She came into my bedroom where I sat on the bed reading *Forever* by Judy Blume. I just started it. All of the girls at school were reading it, so I wanted to be just like them. Auntie Nan was wearing a short-sleeved pale green dress and fleshy pink Kork-ease. She had bright pink toe nail polish on the toes of her tiny feet hiding under her thick sandal straps.

"Annie, why are you inside on such a beautiful day?" she asked as she sat on my bed.

"I like to read. I like to read about other people's lives." In my head, I imagined the conversations I would have with the characters in the books.

"But you should be out with your girlfriends, talking about boys and putting on makeup, Annie. It's a great day. Go outside and soak up the sun's rays."

"I'm happy here. Really, I am, Auntie Nan," I said. I retreated back into my book, touching all of the dog-eared pages.

"Annie, take your book outside," she snarled at me.

Auntie Nan was not really into disciplining us two girls. She didn't understand what it was like to be a husky girl. I was praying for five more inches of height so that I could thin out like all the other girls in my class. Beebee Kimball used to have chipmunk cheeks and she came back from summer taller and thinner. So, did Jennifer Jones. If I get tall enough, all of my problems will be solved.

"All right," I said.

I didn't want to explain to Auntie Nan that I really have no friends and that I like to read in the silence of the house. Gracie was always away at a friend's house. I enjoyed the quiet. Mom sat at the kitchen table staring into her beer can, writing words for other people's music. Daddy didn't sit in his chair anymore, but sat on a barstool down at the Holiday Inn Lounge talking about the only woman he ever loved and how she didn't love him anymore. Nana didn't cook smelly sausage and cabbage that suffocated the air and made me wish for a windy day because Mom was mean to her. She never visited anymore, so a visit from Auntie Nan was like a breath of fresh air.

Auntie Nan walked out of my room with me and walked into the kitchen. I walked back to the door of the kitchen and leaned against the old wooden bookshelves with glass faces that have two-toned book jackets that contained the *Story of Civilization* by Will and Ariel Durant. Mom liked to read about others as well.

"Mia, why don't you take Annie out? Why is she sitting in her bedroom by herself?" Auntie Nan yelled at my mom.

"I have to finish these words, I mean lyrics. This guy wants his words by tonight. Am I supposed to forget about the money and just take her out! Nan, I made a commitment to finish this and I'm gonna finish it. I need the money," Mom said.

"Mia, then I'll take her out. For chrissakes, she's your daughter and it's not healthy for her to be home by herself."

"Fine," Mom said. "Just don't feed her a bunch of sugar. She already has a problem as you can see."

"Fine. I'll see you, Mia. I'll bring her home later."

Auntie Nan walked out of the kitchen and saw me crouching on the floor outside of the swinging kitchen door. She smiled at me.

"Annie, get a sweater. I'm taking you out today. Hurry up." She stood there with a wide smile on her face, and the most marvelous long scarf wrapped around her neck, that almost touched the floor.

I grabbed my sweater and met Auntie Nan out at her car. She had the top down and the car smelled of horsehair. She drove down our street, barely stopping at the sign. Then she ignored the large, black Cadillac that honked at her when she took the right of way. I sat by her in the front seat and watched her hair flutter in the wind. The scarf was wrapped around the back of her neck and around the back of her beautiful auburn hair.

"How you doing, Annie, my star?" She sang to me. Auntie Nan called me her superstar. She had a gift for making me feel special at the moment, although I knew it was not the case.

"I would have been happy at home. You didn't have to take me anywhere." I lied to her. Secretly, I was tickled that I had special time with Auntie Nan. Gracie took all the attention because she was so young and blonde, always showing her dance steps and twirling.

"What is all this from my number one girl? She said smiling. "I need to get another opinion when I go shopping. Anyway, I like to take you out. We have fun, don't we? Always an adventure, that's the way the day should be with me."

I sat in the car smiling at Auntie Nan. We drove across Franklin and continued onto Los Feliz Boulevard. There were big homes made of wood and stone, clean windows with drawn curtains. Warm colors of eggshell and ivory color and smoothe wood, these majestic homes along this wide boulevard have large and happy families sitting at the dinner table talking and sharing the experiences of the day. I sat back and looked at the world through my tinted glasses, a much prettier world. We drove down Hillhurst to Sunset Boulevard and made a left. Auntie Nan pulled into the parking lot of the Akron, the store of rattan and loud prints, of statues and incense. This was where my mother would wheel a cart for hours trapped in her own thoughts.

"Don't worry about locking it up. I'm leaving the top down," she said. "I just want to be free, you know Annabanana?"

"Why are we here, Auntie Nan?" I asked, knowing where we were. Mom had dragged us here last year when she came home and found every plate smashed to bits and Daddy in the bathtub sleeping.

"Because I decided I needed some changes in my apartment. I need some color. A little spice, just a little bit of change, Annie. Shake things up!"

I knew what that meant. Any time Auntie Nan referred to me as Annabanana, that meant she wasn't going to talk about it. Auntie Nan broke up with her boyfriend, Paul. He didn't approve of Auntie Nan's hopes and dreams. He didn't think she should be an actress. Last time I was at her house, I overheard them in the garden talking. He was too ordinary I thought when I met him. Auntie Nan deserved the best. Paul wasn't the best. He just wasn't. He laughed at her when she said she wanted to act. After hearing that, I went back to the bedroom and cried myself to sleep.

I wished I had a magical wand to make all dreams come true. I would make Auntie Nan a star on the Hollywood Walk of Fame. And I would make myself a smaller size with my pretty pink magical wand.

Snapshot
Two Guys from Italy

S itting on the window stools looking at Hell's Angels, I always remembered to not look into their eyes as I was eating my slice. I watched as the girls in the black leather halter tops and blue jeans climbed on the back of their motorcycle beasts.

I rode on a motorcycle once. When Momma and Auntie Bean were still friendly sisters, we would go out to the valley to Auntie Bean's house. Everything was so new and perfect. They all had their own bedrooms and there were two bathrooms. There was a boy's bathroom and a girl's bathroom. At our house, there was only one bathroom.

Uncle Steve seemed like the perfect dad. He was tall and funny and would spin Auntie Bean around the kitchen and dance. I would spin myself around in her sunshine yellow vinyl kitchen chair. Red and Mia just yelled at one another and slammed doors.

On his Harley motorcycle, Uncle Steve rode me around the cul-de-sac on my last visit. That was the last time I saw him. All of that surveying for the 118 freeway, the biggest issue he thought he had was the rattlesnakes. The doctors never could figure out how half of his heart disappeared. He died less than a year later. Whispers of Valley Fever spread throughout the funeral. San Fernando Mission was his resting place, overlooking the 118 freeway. The coffin was closed.

Hush Puppies at the Chateau Marmont

Next door to Norman's studio was the Chateau Marmont. It was a famous landmark on Sunset Boulevard. To get to it, we walked on the street carrying our lunch of soda and chips, with fast cars driving by us even faster, their speed blowing our hair furiously. Obscured by a brick wall and hidden from the entrance, was the pool, our free place, our oasis. No parents fighting, and no adults telling us what to do. We had kid freedom to drink soda and eat chips. We sat on pool furniture inside the gardens and sun patio at the hotel. The terraced brick planters were filled with split leaf philodendrons larger than our heads. No one said boo on Marmont Lane. Electric guitars sounded like they were being beaten up from a window on the second floor. After less than a year of playing a Hawaiian guitar, I recognized the sound of the slide bar.

I'm with my best friend, Dee Dee, and Annie is with us today. Dee Dee's mom, Wendy, her friend, Norman and we three all piled into his convertible as we made our way west of Highland. When Norman had to work on some pictures and needed quiet in his studio, the three of us would sneak over to the hotel pool. The way Norman placed his hand on Wendy's back and body it was obvious they were very close.

In his black Cadillac convertible before working, Norman gave us rides up and down Sunset Plaza where we saw the beautiful silhouettes of little girls' dresses at Holly's Harp. Often, he offered to stop, park and buy dresses for us girls, but I could never accept such an expensive present from someone who was not related to me. On our way to his studio, Norman would run into the Chalet or Greenblatt's at Fairfax and Sunset to pick up food. We stopped at the liquor store on La Brea and then Piece O' Pizza. We only ate pizza from Piece O' Pizza because it was cheesy and greasy, cheap and fast. Driving was different with my family than with Dee Dee's. Some nights when we drove home from the beach and Daddy was sleeping in the front seat, Momma stopped and looked at all of the beautiful dresses at Holly's Harp. She would pull the car over but leave it running while she and I held hands and gazed at the beautiful creations. Annie was asleep from all of the laughing and flirting she had usually done

171

during the day with boys she just met. Window shopping was all Momma ever offered to me, empty promises.

Norman was a photographer from New York City, and his studio was always full of lots of friendly people. One day I met one of the Monkees sitting on a couch talking to Wendy. Later that afternoon Dee Dee asked me to go up and get her jacket. We were not allowed to be among the adults and I awkwardly grabbed the jacket before I was seen, but not before I could hear how friendly Norman and Wendy were with the singer. When I handed Dee Dee her jacket, she started to laugh at me.

"Were they already doing it?" asked Dee Dee.

"I had my eyes closed. I just crept up the staircase without anyone seeing me," I admitted embarrassed.

"They were probably doing it already if it was quiet up there," she said laughing.

Since she already knew what was happening upstairs, I guessed she wanted me to see it. I started to question why Dee Dee did the things she did. I had never even heard my parents, so I didn't want to hear other people's old parents no matter how nice they were.

Once Norman's big black convertible made it up the driveway to the studio, there were no more adventures for the day. Then we had to take a Yellow Cab with Dee Dee's Mom back to our sleepy homes above the Boulevard.

Earlier in the day Dee Dee and I were popping open cans of red labelled Pringles chips and laughing as we made the pool furniture our own jungle gyms and trampolines. Trees surrounded the pool in this paradise above Sunset Boulevard. I felt like I was in the Garden of Eden until the super tanned guy walked over to our pool and laid his sunshine yellow towel on the chaise. Dee Dee looked at me and I looked over at her. His skin was the color of Pioneer Chicken, and it made me grab for more Pringles.

Annie twirled in the deep side of the pool, all alone. She was working at giving herself the spins by continually moving and never stopping. Suddenly, she did stop. There were bubbles blowing out of her mouth as she put her head in the water. Annie seemed to be in a trance, staring in the distance to the other side of the deep end where the chaise lounges were.

I swam across the pool, doggie paddling because I didn't take any class in swimming past the guppy stage. I faced the direction she was facing.

"Yuck!" I said.

In the water Annie was looking in the same direction. Peeping out of the swim trunks of the fried chicken-skinned guy, I saw his two golden balls. They looked just like hush puppies. I swam behind Annie doing my doggie paddling, and she was in some sort of rapture with her mouth in the water. The old guy smiled and looked in our direction. Annie just kept blowing pool bubbles as she stared in the direction of those two perfectly round and sun-tanned balls.

Snapshot
YMCA

Friday nights were the only nights Mom had off for us. We ate out and went for a family swim. I wished I could get higher on the swimming dashboard other than guppy. But in the large, cold pool I would be thrown into by the boys, so I stayed in the small, heated pool where the chlorine smell lingered in my hair for days.

Mom swam back and forth in laps. She never played with me in the pool. I didn't even think she saw me. But every Friday night after she swam, she had a huge appetite. And we went to Two Guys from Italy on Yucca. I got my usual slice and ran my fingers over the red and white checked tablecloth while I ate. When I was done and had to wait for Annie and Momma to finish, I played with the red bubble glass candle.

Annie and Momma were girlfriends. They talked and really listened to each other. I just sat by myself not being talked to and I thought about the walk to school by this place tomorrow. Crazy Mary would be sitting in the doorway and I'll put some gum near her head. "Thanks, kid," she'll say as I run down the block not stepping on lines or cracks.

8x10 Black and White Glossy

Watching the television in the bedroom, I saw the movement of my mother under the bathroom door.

I was in the bathroom watching my mother getting herself ready for tonight. She took the large pink foam curlers out of her hair and teased the crown of her wild red-haired mane. She fingered the tendrils of curls around her face, and then sprayed the Aqua Net. I watched her dab some White Shoulders behind her ears, on her wrists, and in between her breasts.

Finally in Momma's bedroom, I watched her finish dressing in the mirror. I liked to watch her reflection. She was a beautiful woman. I spent my Saturday night looking at her. Underneath her housecoat, she wore shiny black panties and brassiere. I knew this because she slowly took off her housecoat to put on her dress. Then she posed in the mirror, and held her breath. As she made a complete circle, I sat in the doorway.

"Annie, would you zip me up?"

I didn't say a word. She bent over so I could reach the zipper, and I slowly pulled it up. I touched the rich black velvet, so smooth against my hands. I stood on my tippy toes, just to pull it all the way up. She stood up straight and smoothed the fabric around her body. She wore nude stockings, which made her legs even more beautiful.

"You look pretty, Momma."

"Yes, I do, don't I Annie?" She bent down to my height and put her face very close to mine in the mirror. She smiled at our reflections.

"Look at us," I said.

"We look like we could be sisters. I don't think I look old enough to be your mother," she said as she puckered the Fire and Ice red lips.

"No, just like an older sister."

She stood up and walked over to the full-length mirror. She picked up her mascara, midnight black. I always thought it was funny because she opened her mouth when she put it on. Then she placed her rouge in the apples of her cheeks, coral orange. It looked very good against her auburn red hair. And she had this light green eye shadow which made her hazel eyes pop. Then she used the puff on her face and chest. When she was in a good mood, she puffed my nose. But tonight, she was not in a very good mood.

Earlier that afternoon Momma and Nana got into a big argument. Gracie and I were playing with our dolls. My doll is Chrissie. She has red hair, like Mom, and wears a chocolate brown pantsuit with bell bottoms. Gracie has Velvet, a platinum blonde with a purple velour jumper. We were waiting for dinner. Mom slept all day long. When she finally woke up, she stayed in bed and watched television. I went in there and watched "Outer Limits." I like to go in there and place my head against her hip while I watch the television. Mom left the room to get herself a beer. I said I would go get it, like I did for Daddy, but she just left. Usually Gracie climbed all over Mom and I didn't get any special time. But Gracie was picked up over an hour ago for a slumber party. And Mom was in a good mood. Then it started. The house smelled awful. Nana was making sausage, sauerkraut, peas and carrots. And she didn't open the window because it was unsafe here in Hollywood. I listened from the other room.

"Mommy, get off my back."

"You're a mess. You open a beer in front of the girls for breakfast. In front of the girls, you flaunt this man."

"You don't know anything."

"Mia, I did my best. I put everything I had into you."

"You expect me to live like you, Mommy?"

"I did what I could do for you, Mia. I always told you to think nice thoughts. I tried to shelter you from the evil in this world. But you were like a magnet drawn to it."

"You want me to be just like you. Do you want me to be trapped in a loveless marriage for forty years like you?"

Nana and Mom always argued. Mom laughed when Nana spoke about paper thin walls. Nana meant well. I knew that Mom and Daddy used to argue all the time. And then it was quiet. It got quiet when Daddy left. Now Mom and Nana fight. I hate the noise. I hate the loud voices and the angry echoes.

"I loved your father!"

"Look what he did to you. He left you penniless. You had to go and clean other people's homes. And doctors' offices. You had to clean up after strangers. You had to work with your hands."

"It was work and it fed us. It was honest. I didn't sell myself. I knew what I was getting into when I married your father. I wasn't going to stay in that small town. I wasn't going to raise children in that hole. Montana was a hole."

"I'm better off without Red."

"You don't know what is good for you. You should try to make it work, for the sake of the girls. In the eyes of the Catholic Church, you are still married. I stood in front of you and Red while Father Michael said the words. Do you want to have them come from a broken home?"

"Mommy, I'm not going to discuss this with you. This is none of your business. Get out of my business."

Mom came back into the bedroom with her beer in one hand. She got back into bed. With one sip of beer, the wrinkle in the middle of her forehead disappeared. I got off the bed to go see Nana. She sat at the table drinking her Postum out of an old Cream Mate jar. Nana sat talking to herself, until she saw me. She wiped the tears from her eyes.

"She doesn't take care of you girls, like a mother should. I hope she opens her eyes, before it's too late. Always been out for herself and still is. Such a shame, you girls are good girls."

Nana put on her ugly brown sweater, and buttoned it tightly against her stomach. She picked up her two shopping bags, finished her Postum, and left the jar in the sink.

"Annie, I'm going to go now. Your mother will have to call a babysitter tonight. I can't stay where I'm not wanted. I love you girls." Nana kissed me on the top of my head, and then wiped it away with her other hand.

As she kissed me on the forehead, I saw the dirty pores in her nose and her tired eyes hidden behind wire frame glasses that were too small for her face. I saw the dark pink indentations in the sides of her nose where the glasses pinched her. Nana looked sad as she picked up her shopping bag and walked out the door. I watched her walk down the driveway to the street on her way to the bus stop on the Boulevard.

"How do I look?"

"You look so pretty, Mom," I said as I hugged her.

"You're going to be my big girl tonight, right?" she asked pushing me an arms distance away. "I'm not going to have to call you to check up on you, right? You won't have any boys over here, will you?"

"Oh Mom, don't be silly. I'm not even ten."

"I don't like to leave you alone, but you're a big girl now. Your grandmother shouldn't have pulled that stunt today. The only person she's hurting is me! But I'll show her, I'm going out anyway! My customers are expecting me."

Mom stood up and put her lipstick on again. She puckered in the mirror, throwing imaginary kisses at herself.

"You look nice, Mom."

"I do, don't I," she said as she threw her head back.

Mom threw one more kiss at herself and walked out of the bathroom. I followed behind her, suffocated by the perfume bath that followed her room to room.

"I have a surprise for you. Here."

She handed me an 8 X 10 black and white glossy of her in a sexy pose, wearing only a fur coat and sitting on a piano bench. It was signed "Love Always, Mia." It was in a gold frame.

"Just for me, thank you," I said hugging her waist.

"That's a genuine brass frame I got at Pin N' Save, just for you. I was going to wait for your birthday, but tonight is a special night. My big girl is going to spend the night all alone."

"You said you would be back, after your set. Aren't you coming back tonight?"

"After a couple of drinks, I'll be home."

"Just a couple of drinks, right?" I pleaded.

"Annie, don't sound like your grandmother. I'll be back before you wake up in the morning. Now give me a big kiss, but don't wrinkle me or mess up my face."

I barely touched her face before she moved her cheek away from me. She put on the fur coat Daddy gave her, and walked out of the door. I sat in the front room trying to watch television, but I listened to every noise outside. I took the 8 X 10 picture into the bedroom, and left all of the lights on in the house. In the light of my bedroom, I propped the picture up against a pillow and stared at the picture of her. I said my prayers out loud so the noises outside would diminish in my head. And I made a plan. If someone broke in, I'd pretend I dropped dead from fear. I practiced lying very still in bed. Outside I could hear the wind brushing against the dried leaves on the ground. A can danced down the street, as it made a clatter noise. And I lay very still in the bed staring at the sexy photo of my mother, knowing that she would be home after two drinks. This I knew because she promised and gave me her word.

Best Birthday Party Ever

The birthday invitation read "Come to Annie Crocetti's 10th Birthday Party at Fern Dell Park in Hollywood on Western Avenue and Los Feliz. The pink balloons will be directly across from the drinking water station. Come for the fun!"

Momma was so precise about Annie's party. For my parties, she decided a couple of days before and all of the kids from my class came to the party. Of course, it was at De Longpre Park which was very close to school and most of my classmates lived in the apartments that surrounded the park.

Annie's party was amazing. There was a live donkey for the Pin the Tail on the Donkey game (Daddy held up a stuffed donkey and walked it around the party). A clown blew up balloons, and he looked suspiciously like the clown at the Holiday Inn revolving restaurant who made me a pack of poodles the last time we went to dinner.

Annie looked beautiful in a forest green velvet dress and her beautiful chestnut hair in a ponytail on the back of her head with a wide green velvet ribbon. Her birthday outfit was from The Broadway Hollywood. I looked at my stunning older sister and I loved her so much. I loved that she never forgot me and looked out for me no matter what kind of bratty stink eye I gave to her. She was sisterly love.

Momma and Daddy stood on either side of her making her an Annie sandwich as the party sang Happy Birthday. This was the best day ever because there was no fighting or drinking and the police did not come and take Red away.

Ring around the Rosie. Hot dogs on the BBQ. Fishing for crawdads with bare hands. Running around the park up on the bluff in adventures. Fern Dell was the best park for parties and Momma's party plans would be difficult to best. Many parents would try, but Momma was the best party giver ever.

Acknowledgments

To Patrick, who always had the faith in Annie and Gracie, and my writing.

To Riley, who is my amazing girl, living the Life of Riley.

To Grampy D, who has told me his wonderful and unique escapades in Los Angeles and Hollywood.

To Amadea who shared these adventures.

To Auntie Shar, who as my editor and writing mentor has helped me to discover what I meant to write even before I wrote it, whose writing skills are limitless, whose love and guidance are unconditional.

About the Author

A native of Los Angeles, Tara Botel Doherty was raised by her grandmother and mother blocks away from Hollywood Boulevard. She holds an MPW from USC. Now residing in the Santa Clarita Valley with her husband and daughter, she writes regularly about her adventures in Hollywood. *Bread for the Table* was her first novel.

Visit her at: www.taraboteldoherty.com

www.ingramcontent.com/pod-product-compliance
Lightning Source LLC
Chambersburg PA
CBHW070930250626
47159CB00009B/3187